Royally Confused

By

Jill Boyce

Editor: Cynthia Hickey
Book Design by Forget Me Not Romances

This book is a work of fiction. Names, characters, Places, incidents, and dialogues are either products of the author's imagination or used fictitiously. Any resemblance to actual persons, living or dead, or events is coincidental.

But you are a chosen people, a royal priesthood, a holy nation, God's special possession, that you may declare the praises of Him who called you out of darkness into His wonderful light. 1 Peter 2:9 (NIV)

ISBN: 978-1-952661-87-7

Acknowledgments

I praise God, who whispered these stories to my heart and placed the perfect people along my writing path at the perfect time.

I thank my husband, children, family, and friends for their love and support.

Thank you to my mother-in-law, Kimberly Boyce, who beta reads all of my books and always finds the plot holes. You keep my characters from wearing a heavy coat in the summer.

I am grateful to my mentor and friend, Carrie Turansky, for her generous spirit and wisdom, and my publisher, Cynthia Hickey, for believing in my work.

I'm appreciative to Sherri Stewart, my editor for this book, who worked hard to make the story shine and taught me a lot along the way.

I especially thank my mother, who passed away six years ago on the day of my daughter's birth. Her death inspired my first book, *Harte Broken*. She instilled in me the love of books and the desire to dream big. I love you, Mom.

This book is dedicated to Granny Marge who taught me to laugh often and love big. May you still be dancing on top of the washing machines and countertops in heaven.

My hope is my stories will provide comfort, laughter, and encouragement to my readers. May God bless you all.

But you are a chosen people, a royal priesthood, a holy nation, God's special possession, that you may declare the praises of Him who called you out of darkness into His wonderful light. 1 Peter 2:9 (NIV)

Chapter 1
The Ides of March

Dr. Claire Isabel Thomson closed her eyes and made a silent wish before blowing out the single candle on her cupcake. Thirty years old, and what did she have to show for it?

A scrub nurse stuck her head out of an operating room and removed her surgical mask. "Dr. Thomson, you're needed in Operating Room One," she spoke in a clipped accent.

Claire sighed and nodded. "Okay, I'll be right there."

The nurse tilted her head, scrutinizing the dessert. "What's the occasion?"

Claire glanced at the extinguished candle and shrugged. "It's nothing special." She hadn't told her coworkers that she'd brought her birthday cupcake to work because her mother, Mona Thomson, had made her promise to say a birthday wish every year. Since her mother's passing a year ago, Claire hadn't felt like celebrating anything, but she couldn't break a pledge to her mom. Plus, the day didn't feel special. She tossed the cupcake in the bin nearby and pulled out her favorite blue scrub cap covered in cartoon-version

1

golden retrievers from her pocket and tied it around her head.

Washing her hands at the large metal basin, Claire repeated her favorite song in her head two times to ensure she'd cleaned her hands well. She shook off the last droplets of excess water into the sink and muttered under her breath, "Happy birthday to me," before shoving open the metal door to OR Suite One.

The scrub nurse who'd called for Claire raised an eyebrow. "Are you sure you're well? I've seen more chipper faces on my children doing their homework." She handed a sterile blue towel to Claire and stepped back, clasping her gloved hands together.

Heaving a sigh, Claire dried her hands off before tossing the towel to the floor. "Yeah, I'm fine." She shoved her hands into the surgical gloves the nurse held open before her.

"Usually, the prospect of a knee arthroplasty brings a smile to your face. I recall you saying the other day how much you loved doing this procedure because it restored the patient's quality of life. Instead, you look like you're headed to a funeral."

It did feel like one. Losing her mother to cancer last year broke Claire's heart. Still, if her single mother had taught her one thing, it was not to rely on others. Those words echoed in Claire's mind. Her thoughts drifted to a conversation they'd shared years before when Claire was still a little girl.

She'd asked her mother, "Mom, why don't I have a dad? Everyone at school has one. I want one, too."

Her mother patted Claire on the head. "Oh, Claire, my sweet girl, you do have a father. You're a child of God."

"You've said that before, Mom, but what about my real dad? You know, the one you met before you had me?" She lifted her eyes to her mother, yearning to know more—more of who she was, where she came from, and where she belonged.

Mona Thomson gazed down at her daughter, and tears filled her eyes. "You know we don't talk about him. He couldn't be part of your life. Sometimes things don't work out the way we hope they will, and we have to accept it." She whipped her head away and swiped at her tears.

Claire immediately regretted resurrecting the subject with her mother and decided never to mention it again, and she hadn't—not even when her mother lingered in a palliative care home at the end of her illness. She wanted to know so much more about her mother's past but didn't dare bring it up—she didn't want to upset her mother further. Besides, if a father never contacted his child, he must not want her, right?

"Dr. Thomson. Dr. Thomson, do you hear me?" The nurse stood tapping her foot, her head tilted. A quizzical look appeared on her face.

"Hmm...oh, yes. I'm sorry." Claire stepped on the stool to reach her patient. Her five-foot two height posed the only challenge in the operating room. Otherwise, her surgical skills remained the one area of her life in which she had confidence. Surgery provided a safe space. Give her an OR suite or a research lab any day. Leave the public speaking of lecture halls and the uncomfortable pauses of dating to the masses. She didn't need any of it. All she required was a challenging surgical case and her patients. Oh, and Milo, her two-year-old golden retriever.

The case went smoothly, and an hour and a half later, Claire swiped the scrub cap off her head and shoved it in her back pants pocket. She exited the operating room and headed for the cafeteria to grab a coffee. While standing at the self-serve counter, she reached out to grab a paper cup from the stack when her hand brushed against someone else's. Glancing up, Claire found herself staring into the brilliant blue eyes and blond hair of the most handsome man she'd ever seen.

"Oh, I'm sorry. I didn't mean to take your cup. Go ahead, I'll wait," his lilting voice spoke in an upper-crust accent.

She'd lived in the country of Amorley for almost nine months but still found the accent charming. Swallowing hard, Claire's tongue stuck to the roof of her mouth. After a few awkward seconds, she regained her voice. "Um..." *Way to go. Eloquent.* Her eyes flicked toward the cups and lids, and she realized her hand remained frozen over the top one. *Pick up the cup and quit acting like a dork.* She took the top one and set it on the tray before her. Meeting his eyes again, she smiled. "Thanks."

The man glanced at the coffee carafes on the counter and then looked at her again. Raising one eyebrow, he asked, "May I?"

Claire nodded, finally collecting herself. Her cheeks warmed, and she prayed he wouldn't see her heart pounding like a drum inside her chest. "Sure." She tried to pull her eyes away and failed.

He wore a blue plaid shirt under a navy blazer and pressed tan pants with freshly shined black shoes. A coordinating bowtie completed the ensemble. Usually,

Claire would have found the tie pretentious, but he made it look attractive and completely acceptable. Better than acceptable—distinguished. His strong arm reached for one of the carafes and poured the steaming black liquid into her empty cup. The aroma of the dark roast snapped Claire to attention. "Thanks."

His lips spread into a bright smile, and he returned the carafe to its place. "The pleasure is all mine." He extended a hand toward her and introduced himself, "I'm Ethan."

She reached her hand forward to meet his, and the warmth and strength of his touch sent a tingle down her arm. Staring at their hands intertwined, Claire struggled to recall her name. After a second, she pulled her eyes toward his and responded, "Claire. Dr. Claire Thomson. I'm an orthopedic surgeon here."

The handsome stranger's face lit up. "You're the physician who performed my friend's knee surgery this morning. Thank you for taking great care of him. He spoke highly of how well you explained the procedure to him. I believe his exact words were that you were caring and extremely intelligent. What he failed to mention was your remarkable beauty."

Claire suspected her face looked three shades beyond crimson now. Her hand remained entwined with Ethan's, still shaking it. She glanced down at them and reluctantly released his. No sense in him thinking her a weirdo. "Oh, I'm sure he exaggerated, but thank you for the compliment. I love my job. It was my pleasure."

Ethan nodded toward her coffee cup. "You don't drink tea? I thought everyone in Amorley drank it. I'm sure it's a national requirement."

She grinned. "No, I haven't fully acclimated, I

guess. For me, it's coffee or nothing. Tea seems too weak."

Ethan lifted a shoulder. "I cannot agree. Tea helps everything. Perhaps you haven't tried the right one yet." He grinned in a way that made Claire's heart race.

"Perhaps I haven't." People had gathered behind them, forcing Claire to inch toward the register.

Ethan followed behind her, carrying a cup he'd filled with hot water and a still-wrapped tea bag. The line grew, forcing him to scoot closer to her. With the roar of the crowded room, he raised his voice, "Might I invite you to have coffee with me sometime?"

Before Claire could respond, the beeping of her pager interrupted them. She tilted her head down and unhooked the small, demanding device from her scrub pants. Pressing the button revealed the number 2309. *The surgical floor.* She pinched the hinge and replaced it on the waistband of her blue scrubs. "I'm sorry to cut this short, but I have to go. I enjoyed meeting you."

The gorgeous man with a professor-like air extended his hand to Claire. Taking her hand in his, he let his touch linger. "It's been a pleasure. Perhaps we'll cross paths again soon."

Again, she peered at their hands and hated to let go, but the floor needed her, and the reason could be urgent. Releasing his hand, she sent him a final grin. "Perhaps," she spoke softly before turning on her heel and fleeing the cafeteria to call the surgical floor back. *Perhaps.* The thought brought a smile to her face.

~

Ethan watched as the beautiful, petite doctor hurried away. She left him speechless. Her blue eyes reminded him of the water of Maldives, and her blonde hair shimmered down her back in a ponytail that swished and swayed as she left. Her beauty was natural, unadulterated. He liked it. Of course, he'd have to do something about her affinity for coffee over tea, which was ridiculous, but other than that one fact, he could find no other fault.

He recalled his conversation with his friend, Brighton, yesterday. Brighton had tripped and fallen while dismounting his horse during their ride. He'd torn his meniscus, and the surgeon had told Brighton the surgery would be simple.

Ethan hadn't planned to come to the hospital today because Brighton said he likely wouldn't stay overnight. Still, Ethan wanted to ensure that his friend since primary school received the best care. His thoughts drifted to yesterday's conversation as he watched Dr. Thomson leave.

Brighton had pulled back on the horse's reins, slowing it to a complete stop. "When are you going to break down and accept your fate?" He sent Ethan a teasing grin.

Slowing his brown steed, Ethan came alongside Brighton. "What do you mean? What's my fate?"

"Proposing to Lady Abigail Fulton. I overheard our mothers discussing it last week. According to your mother, it's decided. When's the wedding date?" Brighton removed his riding gloves and folded them before placing them in his pants pocket.

Ethan rolled his eyes. "You're joking, right? You know how my mother gossips. Sure, my father would love to see our family united with the Fulton family because of their status, but I've told my parents I'm not marrying for position or money. I even told my mother I may remain a bachelor. That comment made her crazy."

Brighton smirked. "Who are you kidding? You and I are the same—we come from important families, and we must meet certain expectations. You had to see this coming. Fortunately, my older brother's head rests on the chopping block first, so I have a few more years to have fun, but you, my friend—your time is up."

Staring at the horizon, Ethan noted a few clouds rolling in. The previous blue sky had darkened to a hazy grey, and thunder sounded in the distance. He frowned. "My time isn't up. I will not marry Abigail. Aside from not knowing her well, the bit I do know is that she is a flirt and gossip. No, I'd rather shirk my title and face banishment than accept an arranged marriage of that sort." He turned to his friend. "It looks like a storm's coming. Maybe we should head inside." Ethan tilted his head toward the stable just over the next hill.

Brighton nodded.

The two friends rode toward the refuge of the stable and arrived as the first raindrops fell.

Ethan swung his leg off his horse's back and slid to the ground.

"Aah," Brighton screamed and thudded to the dirt.

Circling around the front of Brighton's horse, Ethan peered at his friend. Brighton clutched his right knee with both hands. He grimaced and cried in pain.

"Are you okay?" Ethan asked.

Brighton's face contorted, and he shouted, "No, I'm not okay. If I were okay, I wouldn't be lying on the ground writhing in pain, now would I?"

Ethan raised his palm. "Hey, I'm sorry. I'm trying

to help. What happened?"

"I slid off the horse, and when I took a step, my foot must have caught on a rock or something. I don't know. All I know is it hurts." His friend careened side to side while grabbing his injured leg.

Ethan knelt to help Brighton stand. "Do you think you can put your arm across my shoulder? I'll lift you up, and you can use me as a crutch. It's not that far to the stable door—I think we can make it."

Brighton cringed again but gave a thin grunt, "Okay."

Helping his friend to an upright position, Ethan encouraged Brighton to keep his weight off the injured knee. He grabbed his friend's left side and held on to his right arm, steadying him. Ethan led him slowly, praying their horses would follow. Thankfully, they obliged, and the entire party made it to the barn's haven without further incident.

The sound of the cashier requesting payment for Dr. Thomson's abandoned coffee and the unprepared tea snapped Ethan out of his memory. "I'm sorry, what did you say?"

The woman operating the register wore a white apron tied loosely at her waist. She placed a hand on her hip and nodded toward the line forming behind him. "I said, 'are you going to pay or hold up the line all day?'"

Ethan's neck warmed. "Forgive me…I uh—" he scrounged in his pocket for his wallet, extracted three crisp bills, and handed them to the woman. "Please, keep the change."

She looked at him for a second longer before turning her attention to the woman behind him. "Next," she called.

Ethan picked up his cup and the extra coffee and carried them to a nearby table. He couldn't believe Brighton's injury had led Ethan to this hospital and a chance meeting with the gorgeous doctor. He didn't care about duty or title, not after meeting someone like Dr. Claire Thomson. No, he'd never whisper the name of Abigail Fulton again. No matter what his family said.

Chapter 2
The Ides Continue

Claire checked on the surgical case she'd been paged about, rounded on a few more patients, and dashed to the locker room. She couldn't shake the meeting with the handsome cafeteria goer out of her mind. Feeling her cheeks flush at the thought of his kind smile and blue eyes, Claire shook her head. She'd probably never see him again, and besides, she had important work to do here. No time for relationships or trusting people. No time for getting hurt.

After retrieving her purse and white coat from her locker, Claire slammed the door shut and opened her bag, grabbing her phone. The telephone icon indicated three missed calls. She pressed the home key before pushing the green button to play the missed messages.

"Claire…Claire, oh, I never can tell if this blasted thing is recording or not. Why does everyone insist on using voicemail? In my day, if you called and no one answered the phone, then you called the person back later and—" Her grandmother's scratchy voice cut off as the time expired on the voicemail.

Claire grinned. Good, ol' Granny. She loved her grandmother. Margaret Thomson had helped Claire's mother raise her. Although she stood shy of five feet tall, Granny was a spitfire. Her red pixie haircut clashed with her nearly orange lipstick, but she never left her house without a full face of makeup and a bucket-style handbag slung across her forearm. She told Claire all young women needed a solid leather handbag because it could function as both an accessory and a weapon. Chuckling, Claire punched the button to reveal her next message.

"This silly phone, it cut me off, so as I was saying, I have something to tell you, but it's not the kind of thing to dump on a person over the phone, so I'm coming there to see you. Now, I know what you're going to say—I'm too old to travel to Amorley, my heart is bad, it's not necessary, but this time, it—" The phone beeped, indicating the end of the second message.

Claire imagined her grandmother screaming at the phone and knew before pressing the green button again to whom the third message belonged.

"Ah—I hate these contraptions. I'm coming. Don't bother trying to talk me out of it. I already booked a plane ticket, and I'm arriving at the airport late tonight. I know you'll try to pick me up from the airport, but I don't want to trouble you. You're probably busy cutting people open. Still don't know how you stand to do that, but oh, this thing is going to cut me off again—I'll catch a taxi to your apartment and see you then. If you won't be home, call me back. Otherwise, I'll be there by—" The phone cut off her grandmother for the third and final time.

A glance at the hour caused Claire's pulse to quicken. She didn't want her grandmother to arrive at her apartment before she could get home to greet her. Her grandmother didn't have a key, and Claire didn't want her roaming the hallways alone. First Line Flats weren't known for safety. Also, she pictured the empty yogurt cups sitting on her kitchen counter and cringed. Her grandmother prided herself on her housekeeping abilities, and Claire's didn't make the mark—not even close.

Claire shrugged on her down jacket and knitted hat and dashed out of the locker room, racing for the elevator. Pressing the button, she muttered, "Come on."

The same scrub nurse she'd worked with earlier joined Claire, also waiting for the elevator. She cleared her throat, "In a hurry?"

Raising her gaze from the button, Claire found the nurse's eyes. "Yeah, I need to get home. My grandmother is coming for a visit."

The nurse broke into a wide grin. "Well, that's nice. Maybe she'll celebrate your non-special occasion with you."

Claire sent the nurse a half-smile. "Yeah, maybe."

The button dinged on the elevator and the doors parted. Claire stepped on, and the nurse followed suit. Claire hoped the short trip to the lobby would preclude the need for conversation. She didn't need anyone prying into her personal life. Still, she tried to remain kind.

Now on the elevator, the nurse turned towards Claire. "Where does your grandmother live?"

Claire shifted her weight and stared at the brightly lit buttons overhead, watching the numbers tick downward. "Uh, she's from Boston. In the U.S."

The nurse raised her brow. "Wow, that's a long trip. Is your mother or father coming with her?"

Warmth filled Claire's face, and her stomach

twisted. She stared at her shoes and tried to collect herself. The nurse's question reminded Claire why she tried to keep a distance between herself and her coworkers. With only a few months left of her one-year fellowship at Oxmund University, she didn't want to entangle herself in personal attachments. Halford University—that was the goal, the end game. She'd come here to sneak a glimpse into her mother's past and pad her resume but expanding her social circle didn't make the list.

Noting the nurse's perplexed face, Claire shook her head. "My parents aren't with her. My mom passed away, and my father, well, he's never been around, so—" Her throat tightened. She exhaled when the final button dinged, and the elevator doors opened to the hospital lobby. Claire burst out of the elevator, tossing a wave to her colleague. "Have a good day."

"Dr. Thomson," the nurse called.

Claire stopped and turned, wanting to flee the building. "Yes?"

"I hope you enjoy the day with your grandmother. You're a special person, and you deserve to have a happy birthday." The woman smiled and gave a small wave.

Adjusting the bag on her shoulder, Claire softened. She nodded and allowed a small smile to tug at the corners of her lips. "Thanks. See you tomorrow." Claire turned and headed out the hospital front door and into the frigid blast of the Ides of March. She fumbled with her coat zipper, trying to brace herself for the cold and whatever news awaited her.

Claire suspected her grandmother hadn't hopped a plane and crossed the Atlantic Ocean only to wish her granddaughter a happy birthday. No, Granny had unearthed something big—Claire could feel it in the ache of the wind gnawing on her bones. She wished she hadn't left her gloves and warm leggings in her flat. Shoving her bare hands into her coat pockets, Claire shivered—but the cold wind wasn't to blame.

Claire arrived at her flat thirty minutes later after taking a metro train and walking four blocks to her one-room apartment. Convinced she'd achieved popsicle status; Claire couldn't shove her keys into the lock fast enough. With a turn of the key, the warmth of her place hit her face, bringing with it, relief. Milo came bounding toward her and she scooped him into a hug. Scratching his head, she let him cover her face in sloppy kisses. "Hey, buddy, how was your day?"

He settled down and sat, staring into her eyes. His tongue hung out as he panted, wearing a big, goofy grin. Glancing around the room, Claire realized she'd left it in a worse state than she thought, making her relief at the arrival home short-lived.

Running around the flat, Claire bounced from the kitchenette to the living area, picking up containers of takeout with dirty silverware glued inside them. Claire peeled the forks and knives off the plastic boxes before tossing them in the trash. She really should learn to cook. Every January first, her New Year's resolution list included a pledge to improve her nonexistent cooking skills. Claire only microwaved, had delivered, or picked up her meals. Chinese food remained her weakness, and thankfully within a week of moving to Amorley, she'd found the best Chinese restaurant that delivered takeout to her door in under thirty minutes. *Perfection.*

She opened a cabinet that she'd yet to fill with plates or other personal items and prepared to shove the remainder of her mess inside it. Once open, her eyes tracked to the inside of the cabinet door. A faint carving etched around the edge of the door caught her attention. Tracing her fingers over the words, Claire whispered them to herself, "But you are a chosen people, a royal priesthood, a holy nation, God's special possession, that you may declare the praises of him who called you out of darkness into his wonderful light. 1 Peter 2:9."

What a strange verse to write anywhere, much less on a cabinet. Claire had always attended church with her grandmother as a child because her mom often worked on Sundays. Her mom approached life with a zest for adventure and a love of learning. That love of learning had brought her mother to Oxmund. She'd met Claire's father while studying abroad here in her early twenties. It was one of the reasons Claire had longed to see this place and explore the surrounding countryside. Somehow, Claire hoped she'd find answers here—answers about who she was, where she came from, and why her mother kept everything about that time locked away in her heart.

Her mom had only told her that she'd found out she was pregnant a short time after returning to the United States and had shelved her plans to finish her Master of Public Health degree. Instead, she started working as a research assistant in a local lab.

When Claire asked her mother why she'd never gone back to school, she said it wasn't possible, and she had all she needed in life anyways—she had Claire. As far as Claire knew, her mother never dated. She'd go to work, come home and take care of her daughter, and repeat the process the next day. Mona always wanted Claire to have more in life, so she saved every cent she'd earned, and by the time Claire headed to college, her mother had gathered enough for Claire to attend school debt-free. Thinking about how much her mother had sacrificed caused tears to spring to Claire's eyes. She dabbed them away and shook her head. Fiddling with the edge of her shirt, she realized she hadn't showered or changed. A glimpse at the clock on the microwave reminded her she probably had little time until her grandmother's arrival.

Claire slammed the cabinet door shut and swiped away the remaining tears with the back of her hand. Then, she ran for the bathroom and hopped in the shower. Twenty minutes later, she had used all the hot water and found herself forced to exit her warm cocoon. She dried off with the last clean towel in her apartment and vowed to improve at keeping up with laundry and housekeeping. *Yeah, right.* Well, she'd try, at least.

After tossing a blue sweater over her head that matched her eyes and slipping into a pair of jeans, she hit the light in the bathroom and padded to the kitchen to make coffee. As her hand hovered above the carafe, ready to carry it to the sink and fill it with water, a knock sounded on her apartment door.

Milo had taken his spot on her bed, chewing on a stuffed toy, oblivious to Claire's efforts.

Granny? How could she have reached here so quickly? Claire had convinced herself that her granny would call upon arrival at the airport to check in or confirm directions, but she should have known better. Her grandmother did everything with gusto. Knowing Margaret Thomson, she'd barked orders at airport personnel to carry her items to the front of the airport, hail her a taxi, and load said taxi before they saw her coming.

The knock sounded again, more firm this time. "Hello," a scratchy voice hollered. "Hello, Claire. Are you going to open this door? Hello?"

Claire set the carafe down on the counter and trotted to the door. She swung it open and instantly felt a smile spread across her face. "Granny, it's so good to see you. I wish you would have let me pick you up at the airport. I've been worried about you since I got your message. I could have helped with your bags." Claire peered into the hallway. "Where are your bags, by the way?"

Granny snorted and glanced down the hallway. "Well, they should be here any minute." She lowered her voice to a conspiratorial whisper, "Do you know people drive you in their cars nowadays? No more of those normal taxi cars, or whatever you call it. I've never seen anything like it. Well, anyway, the man who drove me here is bringing my bags up from the car. Although, he did look a little irritated when I asked him to grab them for me—almost as if he doesn't usually do that." She raised her eyebrow.

Claire stepped out into the hallway, praying the driver hadn't run off with her grandmother's luggage. "You can't expect that kind of car service to bring up your luggage. It doesn't work like that."

Her grandmother's brow arched higher. "Nonsense. He's a strong, capable young man, and I see no reason he can't schlep a senior citizen's luggage up two flights of stairs. Which brings me to another point. How in the world do you function in a building without an elevator? Thank goodness you don't live on the tenth floor or something. I'd probably be dead by now from a heart attack from climbing all those stairs." She clutched her chest.

Rolling her eyes, Claire chuckled. "You do have a flair for the dramatic, but I love you. Come inside, and I'll go see what's going on with your stuff."

Her grandmother stepped into the apartment at the same time a young man, probably in his early twenties, appeared. He struggled to carry two suitcases the size of small refrigerators. Beads of sweat trickled from his forehead. Grunting, he heaved the bags on the ground at the doorstep of Claire's apartment. When he'd righted himself, he used the back of his forearm to wipe his brow. Then, he stared at Claire with an expectant look.

Milo ran to greet Claire's granny, jumping up on her leg and nearly toppling her over.

"Milo, settle down," Claire ordered.

The eager canine obliged and sank to the floor at Granny's feet, chewing on the edge of her shoe.

The stranger stood still. Why hadn't he left? Realization struck her and she smacked her forehead. "Oh, your tip. I bet my granny didn't give you one, did she?"

The weary dark-haired man shook his head and sent an exasperated look toward Claire's grandmother. "I tried to tell the lady that's not how the car-share system works, but—"

Claire raised her hand. "Say no more." She glanced over her shoulder to see her grandmother bustling around the kitchen, busying herself with running a dishrag over the counter. Lowering her voice, Claire lamented, "She's not as tough as she looks. My grandmother is a wonderful woman, but you were her first rideshare. I'm sorry." Bending down, Claire rummaged through her purse on the floor. She yanked out two bills from her wallet and stood up to hand the man his tip. "Thanks for making sure she made it up here with all her bags." She sent the driver an apologetic grin, or at least she hoped it looked apologetic.

He accepted the money and shoved it in his front pocket before grumbling something about needing to find a new job. Then, he left.

Claire shut the door behind him, letting her hand rest on the doorframe for a moment before turning to face her guest. "Granny?" She planted her hands on her hips.

Her grandmother stopped cleaning and lifted her head. "Now, don't get started on me. I'm old, I'm tired, and I'll do what I want. Besides, it did that young man some good to hike up those stairs." She wagged a finger in Claire's direction. "Nowadays, young people don't get enough fresh air and exercise. They sit around all day on their devices and barely move. I bet carrying my bags provided him the most movement he'll get today. It probably contributed to his heart health. Maybe saved his life. Who knows?" She shrugged and went back to the task of wiping the counter, this time humming along as she worked.

Claire joined her grandmother and placed her hand on the dishrag to stop its movement. "Are you going to tell me what brought you three thousand miles to see me?" She tilted her head and sent her grandmother a grin. "Not that I'm not happy to see you. I'm thrilled. I've missed you so much, but I figured for you to make the trek, especially on short notice, it must be more important than a sudden need to clean my flat." She settled her eyes on her grandmother's face, waiting for her to spill the reason for the trip.

Granny lifted her eyes slowly to meet Claire's. She searched her granddaughter's face and broke into a grin, but tears flooded her eyes. "Oh, child, come here and hug me. I've missed you, too." Embracing Claire, she seemed to hesitate for a few moments. "Happy Birthday," she whispered in Claire's ear.

"Thanks," Claire murmured.

After releasing her granddaughter, Margaret Thomson wiped away a tear with her thumb and smoothed her bright red blouse. "Why don't we have a seat over there? I have a lot to tell you." She bobbed her head toward the grey loveseat in the living area.

Claire took in her grandmother's appearance. She always wore matching tops and pants—not coordinating but matching, like a red shirt and the same shade of red pants. It almost resembled a tracksuit, but an upscale one. Claire had never given it much thought, but now she found it both odd and endearing. "Okay, let's sit down." Following her grandmother to the sofa, she took a seat beside her.

A long, gold chain with a sparkly rhinestone ball hung from her grandmother's neck, and it swayed a bit as her grandmother got settled.

"What's going on, Granny? Are you okay? Is it your heart?"

Her grandmother waved a hand at Claire. "Pshaw. Are you kidding? This ticker—" she pointed to her chest, "—is the best on the block. I'm a tough, old bird. I'll probably outlive everyone. No, it's nothing like that... it's—" She fiddled with the necklace, causing the ball to roll along the chain. "Oh, I don't know how to tell you… it's—" She cast her gaze to her lap as if considering her words.

Claire prodded, "Tell me. Whatever it is, tell me."

Instead of sharing the news that drove her to hop on a plane and cross the Atlantic, Granny pressed a sealed envelope into Claire's hands. "Here."

Turning the white paper over, Claire noted her mother's handwriting on the front. "For Claire." She flipped the envelope over and saw it appeared to have been opened and then resealed—or at least someone had tried to reseal it. Claire had a suspicion who might have opened it, read it, and glued it shut again. Flicking her eyes toward her grandmother, she whispered, "Is this from Mom?"

Now, her granny's hand froze, and the necklace lay still. She gave a slight nod and, in a soft voice, replied, "Yes."

"Wh—Where did you find it? When did you find it?" Claire asked.

Her granny cleared her throat. "About a week ago. I went to the attic to go through some of your mother's belongings. I wanted to pack up stuff, so you'd have it later and donate the items that didn't seem sentimental. I should have done all this months ago, but it's been hard to look at her things. Last week I decided the time had come, and as I boxed up items from her desk, I found the letter. It had wedged itself into the middle of an old travel book that she must have used when she came here before you were born."

Claire tried to speak, but it felt like her mouth had cemented itself shut. She swallowed hard. "Did you read it?"

Her grandmother frowned. "I'm sorry…I tried not to open it. Told myself I'd wait and give it to you when you came home, but something about the envelope nagged at me. I couldn't leave it alone, so I opened it. Figured if it didn't have anything important inside it, then I'd close it and save it for your return."

Claire chewed on her thumbnail. "It must be pretty important for you to bring it all the way here, huh?"

A breath escaped her grandmother's lips. "Yes."

"Wow. From my mom. Can you tell me what's in it? So, I'm not blindsided when I read it." She lifted her forehead, half not wanting to hear the answer and also praying for the words to tumble from her grandmother's lips like a waterfall.

"It's—it's about your father."

Claire gasped, and her hand flew to her mouth. "My father—but Mom told me he didn't want anything to do with me. She said he wasn't part of the picture, and that was it. Period. I figured he'd left her, left us, and it hurt too much to talk about it. Plus, I thought he must not want me—he never reached out to me over the years. I must not matter to him."

Claire's grandmother shook her head, her hand still clasped around her necklace. "Read the letter. I'll make us some tea while you look over it. Tea helps everything."

Claire traced her fingers along the letters forming her name written by her mother. "That's funny. You're the second person to tell me that today. I never knew tea had such power."

She slid her finger under the envelope's flap and tore the enclosure apart. Pulling out the folded paper, Claire breathed in the familiar lilac and vanilla scent of her mother. Claire's throat tightened, and she felt a pang at the hole the absence of her mother left in her heart.

To my sweet princess, Claire,

I'm writing you this letter because I found out today that I may have only a few more months with you. I spoke with my doctor, and he says I should get my affairs in order. That's what I'm doing.

I'm not worried about you being alone after I'm gone because you'll have your grandmother, and she won't let anyone, or anything harm you. She loves you fiercely. However, I worry that you won't ever see yourself the way I see you—so worthy, so valued. Claire, I haven't done everything right in my life, but I consider you my great accomplishment. You're strong, brave, beautiful, and kind. Don't let grief or anger over what I'm about to tell you tarnish that kindness. Please, don't turn away from God. Lean on him in the coming months. He loves you, too. He finds you worthy.

Where do I begin? I suppose at the beginning. When I spent time at Oxmund University in Amorley, I didn't know anyone. I went there for my education but also to seek adventure. I wanted to find myself. While spending time studying, I met a handsome man at an art gallery. His intelligence, kindness, and sincerity impressed me. I fell in love.

This man and I began dating, and by the

month's end, he proposed to me. At twenty-one years old, I found myself swept up in a fairy tale. That's when he told me the truth about himself; he held the title of Prince of Amorley, and I had accepted a proposal to become his wife and the country's future queen. I was living a real-life fairy tale.

Many young girls aspire to become a princess one day. They dress up in tulle and spin in circles with tiaras on their heads. I never fit this mold. I didn't long to live in a castle and be rescued by a prince on a white steed. I wanted to make my way in the world. I'd planned to get my Master of Public Health degree and then go to medical school. I hoped to save lives and change the world, but I didn't count on falling in love along the way, much less with a prince.

He spoke with his family, and it became clear they did not support the union. Your father's only two options were to marry me and abdicate his position as next in line for the throne—an idea that saddened him because he loved his country and had planned to serve it all his life—or to break our engagement and never see me again.

He told me he still wanted to marry me but didn't want to hurt his family or abandon his country and duty, so we did the only thing we could—we married in secret. We enjoyed a blissful week before his father found out. I'm still not sure who told him because we'd been careful not to be seen together in public, but once he knew, he gave your father an ultimatum—divorce me or give up the throne.

To your father's credit, he'd planned to abdicate and return with me to the United States at the end of my study-abroad rotation. However, I couldn't let him do that. I knew how much his country meant to him, and I couldn't let him leave it behind. I did the only thing I knew to do. I filed for an annulment so the marriage wouldn't show on a public record anywhere, and I told him I loved him but couldn't be part of his world, and he couldn't be part of mine. Then, I left in the middle of the night. I didn't give him a forwarding address or any contact information. It was the hardest decision I've ever made. I loved him, I wanted to be with him, but I didn't fit into the role of princess, and I couldn't let our love destroy his destiny. Maybe I was a coward—afraid to see the relationship through, but that's what I did.

Once I'd returned to Boston, I went back to school as if nothing had happened. I had a month left until graduation, so I applied to graduate school, was accepted, and continued working at the local lab to help pay for classes. Early that summer, I found out I was pregnant. To be honest, it shocked, thrilled, and terrified me. I instantly loved you, but I felt like a kid and didn't know if I could raise one. Thankfully, your grandmother stepped up and supported me. She said it was going to be the three Thomson girls against the world. So, that's what we did. We faced the world on our own, and I never told your father about you.

There, I said it—the secret that's haunted me my whole life. I never told your grandmother who your father was, but rather that I'd had a one-night indiscretion and didn't know the man's name. It killed me to keep the truth hidden, but I thought it would be better for your father to avoid any potential scandal and better for you to stay out of the royal limelight. I wanted you to have a normal childhood. Plus, his father made it clear that he wanted nothing to do with me, so I suspected that sentiment might translate to you.

I never wanted you to feel unworthy. You are more than enough, Claire. You are a princess. Not because of your father's title or birthright. You are my princess, and you are God's beloved. You brighten everything around you. Please, please forgive me. Don't let your light dim with the revelation of this news or because of my passing. I will love you forever and always be proud of the woman you have become. I pray you'll carry these words in your heart.

My dear, sweet Claire, I wanted to leave this letter as an apology but also as an opportunity. I can't decide for you, and I shouldn't have done so years ago, but if you want to meet your father, I'm enclosing his contact information. I doubt it has changed, seeing as his residence is a castle.

I can't tell you whether or not to reach out to him. Avoiding the question of where you come from and who you are can lead to self-

doubt. I never wanted that for you. I know you've always wondered why your father never sought you out or didn't want to play a part in your life. It wasn't his fault. He didn't know. None of his family knew, either. Don't blame them. The blame rests on my shoulders.

I love you. I love you more than you can ever know. Be happy. Take chances. Let people into your heart and make a difference in the world. Know how loved and worthy you are, Claire.

Love and Blessings,
Mom

Alexander Isaac Evercliff, Prince of Amorley
Evercliff Castle
1 Royal Lane
Dorekshire, Amorley 22244

If in Amorley, dial (020)5591-2938 and ask for Royal Affairs. Mention my name, Mona Thomson. The prince will hopefully remember me.

The letter fell from Claire's fingers, fluttering to her lap. She lifted her head and felt her eyes pool with tears. Blinking, several spilled over, and she swiped them away with the back of her hand. Where to begin? She stared at her grandmother and whispered, "You didn't know?"

The older woman slid the rhinestone ball along the chain again with her fingers. She gave a slight shake of the head. "I didn't. Not a thing. Every time I asked Mona about your father, she became upset and changed the subject. So, I left it alone."

Claire studied the black ink from her mother's handwriting, and a few more tears dropped and hit the paper below, causing the words to bleed on the page. She sucked in a deep breath and closed her eyes. Her father didn't know she existed. He might want her. He might care. Opening her eyes, she released the breath and busied herself with folding the letter up before returning it to its envelope.

Her grandmother broke the silence, "What are you going to do?"

Considering her options and the possible ramifications of them, Claire paused before answering, "I'm going to call him…or write to him. Whatever I have to do to see him. I agree with Mom. I don't want to be a princess. That's never been a dream of mine. Let's face it, our family isn't noble." Claire peered at her grandmother and tried to hide a smile. The noblest thing about her family was when her grandmother offered her seat and Bingo stick to Old Lady Pearl because it was the last one available, and Pearl had recently had her hip done. Now that was noble.

Her grandmother's lips turned down. "Why are you grinning? I don't see what's funny about this situation." She arched a drawn-on brow.

Claire shook her head and rose from her seat. "It's nothing, Granny. Why don't we have some tea and go to bed? Maybe a good night's sleep will make things clearer in the morning."

Her grandmother waved her offer away with a flick of her hand and stood. She stretched her arms overhead, her posture partially hunched over from arthritis. "Forget the tea. I'm beat. Let's go to bed." She gave another shake of her head. "A princess! I can't believe you're a princess."

Claire dragged her grandmother's luggage closer to the bed in the one-room flat. She pulled out an air mattress from her pocket-door closet and slid the doors closed. Minutes later, Claire had prepared her air-filled bed for the night and ensured her grandmother felt comfortable in her bed.

As her grandmother pulled the white comforter up to her chin, she gazed at her granddaughter below. "Are you sure you don't want me to take the air mattress?"

"For the last time, absolutely not. I'm not making my seventy-seven-year-old grandmother sleep on an inflatable bed. Besides, you'd never be able to walk in the morning—it would kill your back."

Her grandmother yawned and rolled over. "I suppose that's true. I love you, Princess. Good night."

"I'm not a princess, but I love you, too. Goodnight." This final thought about her royal status and whether she deserved the title or even wanted it drifted through her mind. *A princess*? *Not even close.*

Chapter 3
March 16

Claire awoke early the next day to the aroma of bacon and strong coffee. She dressed quickly and found her grandmother standing at the two-top stove. "Mmm, that smells good, but you didn't have to cook. You're my guest. I should be the one making breakfast."

Her grandmother waved away her concern with a flick of a spatula. "Nonsense. You're my granddaughter, and from the looks of this place, I seriously doubt you've had a home-cooked meal in ages."

Grinning, Claire took a seat at the round table housing two chairs between the kitchenette and the living area. "Thanks." She dug in, and the flavors brought back memories of weekends spent with her grandmother and mom as a child. She'd eat a huge breakfast early on Sunday mornings, and the three of them would chat and laugh until their bellies nearly burst. Then, she'd give her mother a hug and a kiss and see her off at the front door as her mother headed to the lab. Her grandmother would tidy the house before taking Claire to the little brick, white-steepled church two blocks away. Fond memories of those Sundays spent with her grandmother warmed her heart.

After eating, wiping down the kitchen, and picking up a few discarded garments from the floor, Claire had stalled as long as possible.

Her grandmother settled herself on the small sofa and narrowed her eyes, staring at the rumpled clothes in Claire's hand. Shifting her gaze to the closet, she asked, "Are you just going to toss those dirty clothes inside the closet? That's it? What about a hamper?"

"Oh, I don't have space for that. I make a pile on the closet floor, and when it gets too big or I run out of clothes, I take them downstairs in a used shopping bag and do laundry."

Granny's hand flew to her forehead, and her face paled. "I don't know what I'm going to do with you. Your mother never taught you how to keep house, and I don't—"

"Granny," Claire interrupted, "don't you think we can find more pressing things to do today than worry about my homemaking skills?"

Her grandmother snapped her fingers and bolted up from the loveseat. Her long, pink night coat swayed from the sudden movement. "You're right. You need to call that prince. Or maybe he's a king by now. Who knows?" She shuffled around the small apartment in her fuzzy slippers as if searching for something.

"What are you looking for?" Claire asked.

Her grandmother rustled a few things around on the brown coffee table in front of the loveseat. "That letter with his information, of course."

Pulling the letter from within her robe, Claire waved it in the air. "You mean this one?" She grinned.

Stopping the search, her grandmother plopped down

on the couch again. "Hmph." She tilted her head. "Well, go on. Might as well get it over with and give the number a try."

Opening the envelope and retrieving the folded papers, Claire could feel her palms begin to sweat. She stared at the name and address again. Alexander Evercliff—her father. In a few seconds, she could be talking to her long-lost dad. Of course, she doubted the prince would answer his phone. He probably had waitstaff that did those sorts of things. Still, Claire knew this meant she'd taken one step closer to meeting her father, and that thought both thrilled and terrified her. She gulped, and the lump in her throat made it difficult to swallow. "Okay."

Claire stood and crossed the room to retrieve her phone from the nightstand next to her bed. She unplugged it and hit the phone icon. With each digit Claire entered, her heartbeat quickened. She waited as the line rang, placing the phone next to her ear.

"Greetings from Evercliff Castle, on behalf of Her Majesty the Queen. How may I assist you today?" a pleasant, courteous voice resonated through the phone.

Stunned that she'd reached a live person, Claire moved the device away from her ear and glanced at it for a second.

"Hello? Hello?" the voice called.

Snapping out of her disbelief, Claire slapped the phone to her head. "Good—good morning. Hello. Yes, I'm here. I need to speak to—I mean, if it's at all possible, I'd like to talk to the prince. Or king? He might be a king now." Was that snickering? "Uh, did you hear me?"

The woman cleared her throat and became serious.

"Yes, Miss, if I am to understand you, you're requesting a private phone audience with the king. Is that correct?"

Claire shifted her weight. "That's correct."

"Miss, there is no king; however, you must know that if I let anyone who called speak to the ruler of Amorley, she'd have no time left in her day to tend to the needs of the country. Perhaps, a castle tour might interest you. The castle offers them to the public every Monday, Wed—"

Claire interjected, "I don't mean to seem rude, but the prince, or king, or whatever title Alexander Evercliff holds currently, is my father."

This time the voice went mute. After about ten seconds, Claire heard whispering in the background. The woman returned to the conversation with a perplexed tone in her voice, "Please hold for a moment."

Claire listened to a medley of horns and strings until the line clicked. She didn't give the woman a chance to say anything before speaking, "Listen, I know this sounds crazy, but I have a letter from my mother and—"

A different clipped voice came through the phone. "Hello, this is the queen of Amorley. To whom am I speaking?"

Claire's jaw dropped, and she darted her eyes to her granny, who still sat on the couch. She mouthed the words, "It's the queen," before returning her attention to the royal inquisitor. "Um, hi, hello, I'm Claire. I mean, I'm Dr. Claire Thomson, and I believe I may be the daughter of Prince Alexander Evercliff—or King Evercliff. If you're a queen, then he must hold the title of king by now. Anyways, I think he's my father. I received a letter from my mother—her name's Mona, and I think they dated and got married a long time ago, but don't worry, I'm not going to tell anyone about the secret wedding. Then they had me, but I guess she didn't tell him about me, and then—"

The queen cut off Claire's monologue. "My dear, please catch your breath."

"Sorry, I tend to ramble when things make me nervous. Discovering my dad's royal status falls into that category."

The woman's voice lowered, and sadness laced her response, "I understand. Your mother's name is Mona? Mona Thomson?"

Even though the queen couldn't see her through the phone, Claire nodded. "Yes. Was. She was my mother. She passed away a little over a year ago. My grandmother discovered the letter from her with information about my father. I didn't know about him. My mother never told me his name. Are you his wife?"

The Queen's voice thinned. "No. I'm his mother. I'm the queen mother of Amorley, and I'm your grandmother. Your father suffered a tragic accident almost ten months ago and did not survive."

Claire's hand flew to her mouth, and her stomach clenched. She'd never meet her father. "Oh no. That's terrible. I'm so sorry. I—I—I don't know what to say."

Clearing her throat once more, the queen continued, "You don't have to say anything. However, I would like to ask you to do something for me."

Hesitating, Claire ran her robe belt through her fingers. "Um, what did you want to ask?"

"Would you come for a visit to the castle? I'd love

35

to meet my granddaughter, and I could tell you a little more about your father. I'm sure you have many questions."

Peering down at the letter still in her hand, Claire considered crossing the threshold to her past. She could learn about her family and where she came from—but what if she didn't like what she found?

"Please? I know your father would have wanted us to meet. Your call couldn't have come at a better time. I have some important matters to discuss with you."

Claire glanced at her granny. "What matters?"

Granny waved her arms from the couch, but Claire couldn't decipher the intent of the gesturing.

"I think it'd be best if we talked in person. What is your address?"

Claire responded, "My address is 777 Klogsworth Crossing, Dorekshire Province, Amorley."

"That's not too far away. I'll send a car and driver for you. Let's say tomorrow at two p.m. That way, we can have afternoon tea and tour the grounds before nightfall."

Claire repeated the request out loud for the benefit of her granny. "You want me to come to the castle and have tea with you tomorrow at two p.m."

Her granny flapped her arms overhead, indicating Claire should go to the meeting.

"Yes, if you are available," the queen mother answered.

"I don't work in the OR tomorrow, but let me check my schedule for any research commitments. Scanning her apartment, Claire tried to recall where she'd left her planner. She scampered around the small space until her hands landed upon the pink leather book beneath a pile of unfolded clean laundry. "Aha, found it." She flipped through the pages until landing on the current week. Her finger slid down the column next to tomorrow's date, and she saw the box remained empty. "Tomorrow works for me. I'll be ready. What should I wear? It's my first time visiting a castle."

The queen mother gave a small chortle. "I suggest dressing nicely. See you tomorrow." Then, she hung up.

Claire turned to face Granny who wore a mischievous grin. "Looks like you're heading to a tea party. How did she tell you to dress?"

Claire sent her a thin smile. "Nicely. She said to dress nicely—whatever that means."

Rubbing her hands together, Claire's grandmother hopped up again, this time with more energy than before. "Well, then, we have a lot to do before tomorrow. Do you have to work today?"

"No, today I don't have anything planned."

"Yes, you do. You and I are going shopping. We need to find something that hasn't lived on the floor of your untidy apartment for the last month."

Six hours later, Claire trudged up the stairs to her second-story apartment.

Her grandmother huffed and puffed behind her.

Claire spun around. "Granny, are you okay?"

"Yes, yes, dear, I'm fine. Keep going. My ticker might be old, but it still gets the job done." She waved for Claire to continue.

As the duo arrived at Claire's front door, perspiration puddled across the back of Claire's neck. "For a cold day, we sure worked up a sweat."

"Phew. You got that right. I can't wait to get inside and sit down."

The weight of half a dozen bags hanging from her hands caused Claire to adjust their placement so she could find her key and regain sensation in her pinky finger. She cringed. "Why did I let you talk me into buying ten new outfits?" She usually only wore scrubs and workout apparel. Claire shoved the key in the lock and turned it before pushing the heavy door open. Stumbling into the room, she dropped the bags on the floor, took the few steps to the closest kitchen chair, and slumped into it.

Wagging his tail, Milo loped over to say hello to Claire and then turned his attention to Granny.

"Don't you dare jump on me. I'm tired, and my bones cannot take it," Granny told Milo.

The dog gave a groan of displeasure but melted to the floor and rested his head on the ground.

Shuffling across the room, Granny sank onto the couch. A sigh escaped her lips. "I don't recall having to twist your arm too hard on most of those purchases. Besides, you work hard—you should have a few nice things. Not to mention that I doubt scrubs and sweatpants fall into the 'nice castle attire' category." She stared hard at Claire.

Her granny made a valid point. "Okay, maybe you're right."

"I know I am. Now, how about fixing us a pot of coffee and then let's go to bed. You have a big day tomorrow."

Claire nodded. "Okay. Coffee, not tea?" She rose from her seat and started filling the coffeemaker with water and grounds.

"I know how you feel about tea. You're coffee through and through."

Claire chuckled.

Her granny pressed her lips together, growing serious. "I know you have questions about your past and how that makes you who you are, but you must remember something."

From where she stood behind the small counter, Claire raised her eyes to meet her grandmother's gaze. Lifting her brow, she asked, "What's that?"

"I know who you are—you're a Thomson girl, a great doctor, and most importantly, a coffee drinker. Don't you forget it."

Sending Granny a half-smile, Claire poured the dark roast, and the aroma filled the apartment, warming her soul.

Claire and her grandmother chatted about the upcoming trip and how the castle might look. Hours later, they finally dragged themselves to bed. Yes, tomorrow promised new information about her family history, and with her granny cheering her onward, what could go wrong?

Chapter 4
March 17

Ethan pulled on his thoroughbred's rein. Mud caked around the horse's feet from the earlier downpour that had thankfully subsided. Still, it didn't make for an easy or safe ride today. The scent of pine and the fresh, if not cold, air renewed his soul. He loved this—being outdoors, away from the trappings of his family's estate and all the expectations that came along with it, namely Abigail Fulton. How could he marry her? He couldn't. Sure, her family had a lot of power and wealth, but didn't love count for something? He'd tried to explain this fact to his mother and father again last night over dinner. The conversation had ended in a quarrel, and his father had stomped off to his study.

His younger brother, Richard, arrived next to him and pulled his dark horse to a stop. "Are you going to sit there all day?"

He peered over at Richard. His brother stood two inches shorter than him, a fact that drove Richard crazy. To compensate, his brother often challenged Ethan to competitions, whether it be riding, jumping, fencing, mathematics—nothing remained off-limits. Richard had mentioned more than once that he'd had his eye on Abigail, and if it were up to Ethan, he'd bless that union tomorrow. However, as Earl of Abbingdon and heir to the Kane fortune, Ethan had responsibilities. At least, that's what his father constantly said.

"Hello? Ethan," Richard spoke.

Ethan snapped out of his mulling and shook his head. "I'm fine. I couldn't stop thinking about what father said last night."

"What's that?"

"That I'm to make a proper proposal to Abigail Fulton by the month's end."

"Would that be so terrible? She's gorgeous, powerful, and wealthy. What's the problem?"

He rolled his eyes at his brother's simplification of the situation. "You know the problem—I don't love her. I can't marry someone I don't love."

"Then step aside and let me have a chance at winning her heart."

"That would be fine by me, but you know how father talks about our futures—like stock options. He says I have to marry first, and he's determined Abigail as the best match because of her father's money and position in Parliament." Ethan didn't add that since his unexpected meeting with the beautiful doctor at the hospital, he couldn't get her blue eyes and bright smile out of his thoughts.

Flipping the reins to the other side while holding them in one hand, Ethan shifted his gaze ahead. Storm clouds gathered overhead, and a low rumble of thunder sounded. "Perhaps, we should head back. It looks dark over there."

Always rash, Richard, sent him a challenging look. "Why? Does a little thunderstorm scare you?"

"It's not that, Richard. Think of the animals." As if

to prove his point, Ethan's horse began stomping his feet.

Richard sneered. "You can do what you want, but I'm riding." He gave a sharp dig into the horse's sides with his heels. At the same time, lightning struck a tree nearby. The crack resounded, and both their horses bolted.

With wind and rain spattering Ethan's face, he made a promise to himself—once he regained control of his horse and tucked him safely inside the stables, he would have strong words for his brother. The wind picked up, and a strong blast caused another tree to fall in front of his path. Ethan's horse rose on his hind legs, but he hung on with every ounce of strength within him.

Praying for the horse to settle down, he fought to stay on the steed. Within seconds, that hope vanished, and he slid off the back, landing on the ground with a thud. His horse took off, determined not to stick around for tree number three to fall.

As Ethan struggled to a sitting position, he lifted his eyes and saw he'd landed near the local road. His feet lay safely on the grassy area next to the road, but his upper half edged onto the pavement. He pushed his damp hair out of his eyes and squinted. Was that a limousine coming his way? Narrowing his eyes further, he confirmed his suspicion. A long, black limousine zipped along the road and stood only twenty feet away. He flailed his arms, praying the vehicle wouldn't run over him.

The screech of brakes met his ears, and he heaved a sigh of relief when the car halted a mere foot from him.

The driver wore a cap and a terrified expression. He

assumed the driver might come to his aid, but instead, the rear passenger door opened, and Ethan couldn't believe who emerged.

"Ethan?" The willowy, blonde doctor he had met at the hospital approached him, holding an umbrella over her head. She looked like an angel—well, an angel wearing a royal blue knee-length coat and black heeled boots.

"Dr. Thomson? What are you doing way out here…in a limousine?" Ethan tried to push to a standing position, but pain seared his brain when he put weight on his right ankle. He grimaced. Thankfully, the rain shifted to a light drizzle and then stopped as suddenly as it began.

The angel closed the umbrella and asked, "Did you get hurt?" Her forehead creased as concern filled her eyes. She bent lower, set the umbrella down, and surveyed his legs. "May I take a look?"

He stared into her eyes, reminding him of the ocean his family had visited once as a child. Ethan could get lost in them. Easily. "Sure."

After a few maneuvers, she released his foot, picked up her umbrella, and stood. "It's only a sprain. Still, you need to stay off it for a few days and let it heal. Keep it elevated and ice it." Her gaze took in the whole area, and her brow furrowed. "How did you wind up in the road?"

Before Ethan could answer her question, Richard trotted up and spoke for him, "Whoa. Whoa, boy." He pulled his reins back, stopping his horse. "Looks like you lost your ride there, Ethan."

Ethan scowled and attempted to dust some of the muck off his pants before meeting his brother's smirk.

He read contempt there. "Thanks for your concern."

His brother rolled his eyes. "What happened? Did you fly off? How many times do I have to tell you to hold onto the reins?" Of course, Ethan's horsemanship and the presence of a beautiful woman would bring out Richard's competitive spirit.

Ethan frowned and defended himself, "Well, I find it easier to stay on horseback when my brother listens to my warning of an approaching storm." As if to emphasize this point, another round of lightning cracked in the distance, and Richard's horse started to high step.

Worry painted Richard's face for several seconds. After a few reassuring words to the animal, his brother regained control, and his usual overconfident countenance returned. His attention shifted to Claire. "I'm sorry, I've forgotten my manners." He dismounted the horse and stretched his hand toward the doctor. "I'm Richard, Ethan's younger brother, and the Bar—"

Ethan couldn't listen to his snobbish brother spout off all his titles, courtesy or otherwise, so he raised his hand toward him. "Richard, would you mind helping me stand up?"

His brother appeared annoyed at the interruption but obliged, taking a few steps closer and bending down to offer his arm to his older brother.

Once standing on one foot with an arm draped across his brother's shoulder, Ethan settled his eyes upon Claire. He nodded toward the limousine. "I apologize for the inconvenience. It looks like you were on your way to something important."

She glanced over her shoulder at the car waiting for her return and then faced Ethan again. "I guess you could say that. Do you need a ride? I'm on my way to the— "

Richard waved off the offer. "No, thank you, Miss?"

Pushing a strand of honey-colored hair behind her ear, Claire supplied her name, "Claire. Dr. Claire Thomson. Ethan and I met the other day at the hospital."

Richard dipped his head toward her. "Dr. Thomson. It's been a pleasure making your acquaintance, but I assure you I will take care of my brother. We can both ride on my horse to the stable, and I'd wager that his horse will arrive there before us. They're great at finding their way home."

The pretty doctor smiled at the two brothers. "Okay." She extended her hand to Richard and gave it a shake. "It's been nice meeting you, Richard." Her eyes flicked toward Ethan, and she gave him her hand, too. "Ethan, great seeing you again. Take care of that ankle, and if it doesn't feel better next week, come see me at the hospital."

Ethan allowed his fingers to linger on hers for a moment longer than necessary. He'd never seen such a gorgeous woman. Realizing he still held her hand in his, he released it and sent her a wide grin. "I will. Thank you." He watched her walk toward the automobile waiting for her and prayed this wouldn't be their last meeting. Ethan didn't know how or where, but he hoped he'd see Dr. Thomson again soon. Pulling his eyes away from her retreating figure, Ethan shifted his attention toward his brother.

Richard lifted his eyebrows. "Ready to go?"

He didn't want to tear himself away from the

enchanting doctor, but the storm might worsen, and he needed to find his horse and attend to his ankle. Instead, he obliged, "Sure, let's go."

Chapter 5
March 17

As the limousine bumped along the rough, rocky road, Claire pondered her chance meeting with Ethan. She couldn't shake his handsome image from her mind. Her cheeks warmed as she considered his kind smile, piercing blue eyes, and strong jaw. She recalled the fragrance of his cologne—a blend of sandalwood and spice, a manly scent.

The driver rolled down the partition window and called over his shoulder. "Miss, we're nearly at the castle. I wanted to let you know so you could prepare."

She wondered what she needed to prepare for but instead replied, "Thank you, sir." The road changed to elegant stone pavers, and two minutes later, the car stopped in front of a guard station. An attendant stepped out, wearing a tall hat with a feather plume on top and a military-style uniform in royal blue. A gold sash crossed his chest, and he held a sword by his side. Marveling at the pomp and circumstance, Claire felt her jaw go slack.

The attendant bent at the waist but said nothing.

Rolling down the front window, her driver greeted the guard, "Hello, I have Dr. Claire Thomson here to see the queen mother."

The attendant stepped back to his hut, remaining silent, and opened the gate ahead of them.

Her throat went dry. She hoped she'd remember how to speak once inside.

The car rolled along the driveway and came to its final resting place in front of the towering stone-clad palace. Exiting the car, her driver came to her side and opened the door for her. "Welcome to Evercliff Castle."

Whoa. Before her stood a real castle. She suspected it had a moat and everything. Claire stepped out of the car, and another attendant appeared at her side.

This one wore a black suit with tails and a dress shirt underneath. His shoes gleamed, and white gloves donned his hands. He dipped his head and introduced himself, "Miss, I am Albert, the master of the Evercliff household. Please follow me. The queen mother is expecting you." He straightened and sent her a thin smile before leading the way toward the palace.

Following Albert, Claire took in her surroundings as she made her way to the castle's front door. The exterior consisted of a stone façade and turrets that stretched to the clouds. A round tower divided two courts. The central area boasted hundreds of yards of green grass, perfectly trimmed in an alternating pattern.

Staff wearing black pants and blazers lined the staircase to the front entrance. They looked official but more understated than Albert.

He walked past the welcome committee and looked over his shoulder at Claire. "This is the Grand Entrance. It stands nearly forty feet tall. We recently refurbished it, so although the wood is hundreds of years old, it remains in excellent shape." He beamed as if he'd done the restoration himself.

"It's lovely...impressive, really. I've never seen anything like it in my life—not too many castles where I'm from." She gave a nervous chuckle.

"No, I'd imagine not. Well, follow me. You're going to take tea in the drawing room. It's magnificent. The tapestries are almost nine hundred years old." Albert continued with his tour while leading her to her final destination.

The closer she came to meeting her mystery grandmother, the more her palms sweat.

Albert stopped at the entrance of a room with tall windows flanked on either side with sapphire draperies lining one wall. In the middle of the room sat a rigid figure in a golden chair. The seat next to the person remained empty. He turned to face Claire and asked, "May I take your coat?"

She nodded and removed her jacket, handing it to him.

Leaning in, Albert dropped his voice to a whisper, "Now, this bit of information is important. When you meet the queen mother, you address her as Your Majesty and give a small curtsy." He pulled his head back and surveyed Claire before tilting his head closer again. "You do know how to curtsy, don't you?"

Of course, she didn't know how to curtsy. She spent eighty hours a week standing on a stool in an operating room. Give her a knife and a bone drill any day. This royal protocol stuff seemed ridiculous. "Uh, sure." Hey, she'd figure it out. How hard could it be to curtsy?

He stared at her for a few seconds as if trying to ascertain if she had told him the truth before giving a slight nod. "Very well. Let's get on with it." He entered the room, and Claire followed him once more.

Claire rehearsed her introduction in her head several times as her steps closed the distance between her and her long-lost grandmother. Once she stood facing the queen mother, she found herself fiddling with the cuff of her sleeve, not knowing what to do with her hands.

Albert broke the tension with his introduction, "Your Majesty, may I present to you Miss...Lady...Dr. Claire Thomson." He bowed at the waist and stepped back.

The queen mother lifted a pair of glasses from the accent table next to her chair and placed them on her nose. "Thank you, Albert, that will be all. Oh, except, would you let the kitchen staff know we will have our tea in fifteen minutes?"

"Of course, ma'am." Albert dipped his head and spun on his heel, exiting the room.

Now alone, the queen mother narrowed her eyes as if inspecting her newfound granddaughter. "My dear, please, take a seat."

Claire racked her brain as to what a proper curtsy might look like before settling upon a pose from her kindergarten ballet class. She tucked one foot behind her and presented her hands forward and low, bowing her head. She probably looked like she'd performed a rendition of *The Nutcracker*, awaiting her final curtain call. "Your Majesty."

Her grandmother clucked her tongue. "Now, now, stop that. You are my granddaughter, the daughter of my son, Alexander, and thereby you are royal, too. Take your seat."

Claire obeyed and replied, "Yes, ma'am." She'd heard Albert say it, so it must be okay. Plus, her mother always told her to say yes, ma'am, and yes, sir. Good manners mattered. She scooted closer to the gold chair next to her grandmother and planted herself in it.

Her grandmother gave her a stare. "Now, let me look at you. How old are you?"

Smoothing her dress, Claire wished she could make her hands stop sweating. "Uh, I'm thirty years old. I celebrated a birthday a few days ago."

"Hmm, I see. Are you working here? You sound American, so I assume you don't live here permanently. Did you move here?"

"I'm, um, I'm doing a specialized fellowship and research in orthopedic surgery—a new knee surgery technique. It's fascinating. Did you know that the knee has—"

Ignoring Claire's medical monologue, the queen mother persisted, "Yes, but where are you from in the United States?"

"I'm from Boston. I grew up there and lived with my mother and grandmother. Well, my other grandmother, but at the time she was my only grandmother because I didn't know about you, and I know I'm rambling, but—"

"My dear, you must calm yourself. Speak slowly and thoughtfully. We're going to have to make you ready by the month's end. In that case, our work begins today."

What work did her grandmother mean? Before she could ask, another person arrived carrying a large silver tray filled with a teapot, two china cups and saucers, a creamer, and a sugar bowl. Another member of the waitstaff followed behind the first young girl. A gentleman, probably in his fifties or sixties, brought a wooden box. It lay open in front of his chest, revealing at least a hundred different types of teas nestled on a bed of royal blue velvet. *How many people did it take to run this place?*

The younger woman with the tray lowered it before Claire.

Claire nodded at the attendant as she took her teacup in hand. She thanked the girl for it. Lifting her eyes to her grandmother, she smiled. "Thank you for having me today. I've wanted to know about my father since I was a little girl." Claire raised the cup to her lips and took a cautious sip of the hot liquid. It warmed her soul and calmed her nerves a bit.

The queen mother peered at Claire over the top of her cup and took a drink but remained silent before placing the teacup back on a saucer in her lap. "I'm thrilled to have found you because we have an important matter to discuss. You see, If I don't name a new heir by the end of the month, then the Crown may go to your stepbrother. I'm hoping you'll consider the position."

Claire furrowed her brow. "Wait. What? What do you mean? Why would I become queen of Amorley? I just want to know more about my father, not become the next queen. Why would it be such a tragedy for the Crown to pass to my stepbrother?"

Her grandmother pursed her lips. "A tragedy— perhaps not a tragedy, but not an ideal situation. When your parents' relationship ended, it broke your father's heart. He did not marry for love the second time. It seems he considered your mother his soulmate and resolved to accept his responsibility to the country by marrying for position the next time."

Claire frowned. "I see."

Her grandmother nodded and continued, "His father, your grandfather, wanted him to wed Maurelle because her family ruled the country of Luchtenberg. At the time, her family had immense wealth and political importance. Tensions between our countries ran high, and your grandfather thought a marriage between the two would smooth things. Since then, however, your stepmother's country has crumbled, and the wealth has dissipated. As a result, I fear she has set her sights on obtaining total control of Amorley."

"Oh my." Claire didn't know what to say next. She glanced down at the cup in her lap as if it might provide answers. "Maybe my stepbrother would make a good ruler."

The queen mother's gaze shifted toward the window. Her eyes returned to Claire's, and she placed her cup and saucer on the table next to her. "He's not an unkind boy but he doesn't have a strong mind of his own. I fear his mother would be the one in charge." Then she rang a bell, and within seconds, an attendant returned to retrieve their teacups. The queen mother turned to Claire and rose, indicating that teatime had ended.

Claire followed suit and stood, clasping her hands behind her back so that they wouldn't shake. "Your majesty, I mean, ma'am, I don't know what you exactly want from me."

Her grandmother sent her a small smile. "Come with me." Then, she exited the room.

Claire didn't dare ignore an order from a queen, so she walked behind her grandmother out of the drawing room and down a long hallway. Their heels clicked against the marble floor, sending echoes down the corridor. At the end of it, another door opened as if on command, displaying the most beautiful garden. Being early spring and still cold, flowers had yet to bloom, but the shrubs, bushes, and trees looked green and tidy. "Wow, this garden looks stunning. I can only imagine seeing it in summer. I bet the flowers smell lovely." Claire scanned the grounds for a few seconds before turning her attention back to her grandmother. It still felt weird calling a queen her grandmother.

The queen mother inclined her head. "Yes, I'm quite proud of the Royal Garden. Over five hundred different types of flowering trees, shrubs, and plants live here. We have ten head gardeners on staff and a full team of grounds people. "Let's take a stroll, shall we?" She didn't wait for Claire's reply but walked forward, her below-the-knee skirt swaying with the brisk March wind.

Claire noted that the queen mother wore the same type of stockings her American grandmother used for Sunday morning church services. However, Claire suspected the queen mother's nylon stockings cost a bit more than the ones her granny popped out of an egg-shaped container.

After a few minutes of walking in silence, Claire's grandmother stopped by a large bush with new redbuds. "Claire, look at this rose bush. What do you see?"

Claire stared at the green orb sprinkled with the occasional glimmer of red life and pondered the point of this exercise before answering, "Uh, an undeveloped shrub?"

"Hmm...well, you're partly correct. This rose bush has resided on these grounds for many years. Despite harsh winters, frigid spring frosts, and the occasional wildlife nibble, this plant continues to bloom. You can't see what it is to become yet, but that doesn't mean the potential's not present. These small buds trying to open up will soon display their true worth and beauty to the world—in a few short weeks even."

"Wow, that's a lot of expectation for one bush."

Her grandmother caught Claire's eyes and stared evenly. "It is. However, I don't think I've misplaced my expectation. Like this rose bush, I believe you too can bloom in a short time and be ready to present to the country and the world as Amorley's future queen—the rightful heir to the Crown."

Claire stared at the bush, afraid to meet her grandmother's eyes. *Queen? Her?* How could she leave her fellowship? It sounded crazy. What did she know about being royal? Still, the prospect of learning more about her father and the royal family nagged at her. "Me? A queen? I don't know, ma'am, I'm not the princess type. When all the little girls in my kindergarten class dressed up in tiaras and fancy dresses, I put on a white coat and made a pretend clinic. I'm not even sure I'd want to become a queen."

The queen mother enveloped Claire's two hands in hers, and the action took Claire by surprise. "If you agree to come to stay at the castle for a month, then I promise to teach you everything you need to know about being royal. I'll share stories of your father with you and answer any questions you have about our family. Then, if at the month's end, you don't want to accept your birthright, I'll wish you my best and understand your choice. However, I'd love the opportunity to spend some time with my granddaughter and to teach you about my country—a country filled with people I love and adore serving. I think you could come to love Amorley and its people, too."

Claire pulled in a deep breath and held it. She lifted her eyes to the sky and said a silent prayer. *God, help me to know what to do.* When she met her grandmother's gaze again, she gave a small smile. "I don't know, ma'am. Could I take a day to think about it? I'll need to speak to my fellowship director and see if I can take a leave of absence. Oh, and my other grandmother arrived in the country a few days ago. Could she come with me if I decided to stay for the month? She's not in good health, and I hate to think of her on her own in a country she doesn't know."

"Hmm…both of you here…well, I don't see why not. You sleep on the decision for the night and let me know tomorrow. You can leave word with the royal operator. If you decide to come, I'll send the car for you again."

Claire glanced at her watch. "Okay, I'll let you know. I'm sorry to cut our visit short, but I do need to get home."

Her grandmother nodded. "Let's head to the house, and I'll have Albert call for the driver. Please think about what I said. This could be a chance for you to learn about your family. I don't doubt you'd make a better ruler than Maurelle and her son."

Claire raised an eyebrow. "Really?"

"I try to believe the best about others, but sometimes I don't know—" Claire's grandmother headed toward the castle again, lost deep in her thoughts.

Claire followed behind, but as they arrived at the back entrance, she stopped the queen mother.

"Grandmother, or Your Majesty, or, uh, I mean, ma'am, may I use the Royal Restroom?"

A hint of a smile tugged at the corner of her grandmother's lips. "My dear, ma'am, will do fine, and they are called washrooms—nothing royal about that, I suppose."

"Oh, right." Claire imagined her face had turned three shades of crimson.

"You may use the guest washroom three doors down on the left. While you freshen up, I'll tell Albert to prepare the car."

Relief coursed through Claire, and she sent her grandmother a grin. "Thanks." She made her way to the bathroom and tossed some water on her face to calm herself down. All of this seemed like too much—too much information, too much change, too much family mystery, too much drama. Why had her mother hidden the past from her only to leave her to sift through it like this? She patted her face dry and stared at her reflection for a few seconds before placing her hand on the door to leave. "Oof." She bumped into a tall woman. "I'm sorry, I didn't see you there."

The raven-haired woman had piercing emerald eyes, arched brows, and porcelain skin. She wore a black pantsuit that cut her figure in a flattering way. Three-inch black patent leather heels further emphasized her height, and her commanding presence towered over Claire's petite frame.

She opened her ruby lips and responded, "No need to apologize. I don't believe we've met. I'm Maurelle Evercliff, the queen." She extended a hand to Claire.

As Claire shook it, she couldn't tear her eyes away from the queen's spindly fingers. They looked like spiders. She shivered. "It's nice to meet you. I'm Claire. Dr. Claire Thomson, um, the king, your husband, well, he's my father. Or he was my father. I only just found out."

The queen's eyes narrowed into slits like a serpent. "Oh. Well, Dr. Thomson, the pleasure is all mine. What a delight to meet the offspring of my late husband. I hope you've enjoyed the grand tour."

"Yes, the queen mother, I mean, my grandmother—she showed me around. She asked if I'd come and stay for a while."

Maurelle's mouth dropped open. "Oh, she did?"

Claire nodded. "I'm not sure I want to leave my medical endeavors right now, but I told her I'd consider it." Her nerves caused the words to tumble out before she could stop them.

Her stepmother's lips pressed together. "Hmm, yes, well, I imagine working as a physician requires a lot of time, so we'd all understand if you can't come. Now I must attend to some important business for one of my charities. Again, I'm glad to have met the king's daughter."

Claire started to open her mouth, when Albert appeared at the queen's side. A breath of relief escaped her lips. He'd saved her from further intimidating conversation with her stepmother.

Albert's eyes darted toward the queen and then scanned Claire's face. He seemed to surmise the situation quickly. "Dr. Thomson, are you ready to leave? I've called for the car, and I believe it has arrived." He extended his arm to Claire, and she gratefully accepted it.

Her eyes shifted to her stepmother. "I guess I should

go." Claire moved past the queen to exit the castle.

As she started down the hallway toward the front door, the queen called from behind. "My dear, do take care. Sometimes the castle can cause you to lose your way. Watch your step." This final piece of advice felt more like a threat than a concern. The queen turned and strode away, her high heels clacking against the floor with ominous echoes.

Claire followed Albert to the front entrance and down the stairs to the waiting car. She slid inside, and for the first time in several hours, her shoulders relaxed. The queen's warning resonated in her mind. *Watch your step.* Claire suspected if she came to the castle to stay, she'd have to heed Maurelle's words.

~

Claire sat down at the table near the kitchenette with her granny. They shared a snack of scones and spent the evening going over the day's events at the palace.

Granny Margaret wanted all of the details. She loved hearing about the castle and the grounds, especially the garden.

When it came to the topic of Maurelle, Granny didn't hold back. "I can't stand manipulative people. She threatened you! That's what she did—a poorly veiled threat at that."

"We can't assume she meant it as a threat, but she didn't exude any warmth. Perhaps it's just her way, but let's not focus on her right now. I have a big decision to make. What should I do?"

Granny scrunched her forehead. Her red plastic glasses slid down her nose, and she pushed them back into place with her finger. "Well, you have two choices—turn down Royal Camp or take a chance and say yes to the castle. Hey, isn't that a television program?" she asked, a teasing tone in her voice.

Claire planted her hands on her hips and cocked her head to the side. "Come on, Granny, this is serious."

Rubbing her hands together, her grandmother bobbed her head. "You're right, okay. Let's see…so if you go to 'Royal Lessons,' we both move into the castle and get a month-long vacation. Sounds pretty good to me."

"A vacation for you—I'll be learning how to curtsy and drink tea and how Parliament works with the Crown." Claire took a bite of her blueberry scone—one of her favorite things about Amorley.

Digging into her strawberry jam on toast, Claire's granny took a nibble and wiped the edge of her lip. "If you turn down the queen mother, then you get to finish your fellowship and return home to Boston to that fancy, highfalutin job at Halford University. You've always dreamed of working there. Plus, you love surgery. What are you going to do about that if you become queen?"

Claire considered this point as she chewed. After swallowing, she answered, "I don't even know if they'll want me to become queen at the month's end. I might do a terrible job, and they'll send me home. Even if they do offer the position to me, I don't have to accept it, right?" She raised a brow.

Nodding, her grandmother pointed her toast at Claire. "Right."

"I would like to learn more about my father. I've dreamed about it my whole life—to know him. Now, I have a chance. Maybe I should do it."

Rising from her seat, Granny picked up her empty plate and took Claire's as well, carrying them to the kitchen sink. After placing them inside, she met Claire's gaze. "Maybe you should. Do you want me to pray for you?"

Touched by her grandmother's sentiment, tears filled Claire's eyes. She nodded. "That'd be great."

Her grandmother bowed her head and spoke softly, "Father God, please give my sweet Claire the wisdom to know what to do. Help her determine if she should pick a stethoscope or a tiara. Amen."

Her grandmother had a way of simplifying the situation, didn't she? Claire faced a choice between medicine and royalty, but she also had the opportunity to learn about her father, which tilted the scale toward the castle. Something about the mystery behind the man she never knew tugged at her heart. When she raised her head from the prayer and opened her eyes, she had her answer. "I'm going to do it. I don't know what my fellowship director will say, but hopefully, I can convince him to give me a month's leave. Either way, I have to discover more about my dad. Will you help me prepare? I'll need to pack enough outfits and shoes for almost a month."

Granny Thomson snapped her fingers and did a little jig in the kitchen. "Wahoo! We're going to stay at a castle. Watch out, Evercliff. Granny's coming to town."

Claire shook her head and chuckled. "I'll call the queen mother tomorrow."

~

The next day, Claire surmised the queen mother had no idea what she'd done by inviting Margaret Thomson along, too. The following weeks would be interesting. Claire dropped another load of shopping bags in front of her apartment door. She blamed her grandmother's influence. Every time Claire picked up a new blouse or dress, Granny immediately barked, "Buy it." Four hours and at least a dozen bags later, they'd bought out the entire Dorekshire Square Mall.

She pulled out her key and unlocked the apartment, her grandmother following behind.

Granny hummed a tune from the fifties as she entered the room. She'd worn another one of her monochromatic outfits today—a pair of green polyester pants with a matching emerald blouse. Even her loafers coordinated in a similar emerald hue. "Well, I think we're set. Now, we need to cram all this stuff into luggage, and royal life here we come."

Dragging the sacks into the apartment, Claire placed them next to the kitchen table and headed for her closet. "I have at least two or three suitcases we can use." She yanked out two medium bags and one large tattered black piece of luggage from the back of the closet and heaved them onto the bed. "Here, these should do."

Her granny pressed her lips into a thin line. "That's your luggage? It looks like you're heading out on a European, pre-college, finding-yourself trip. Those aren't suited for a castle."

Claire stared at the worn bags and shrugged. "Well, they'll have to do because it's all I have."

Shaking her head and tisking, her granny remarked, "Reminds me of the time Old Lady Pearl brought that cake to the church bake sale in a tin from 1902. Who would buy a cake in an ancient, banged-up pan? No one, that's who. Did she listen to me? Nope. Never sold that cake."

Claire settled her eyes upon her grandmother and spoke with a warning tone, "Granny—it's fine. I'm tired, and we leave tomorrow for Evercliff. It took almost all of my energy begging Oxmund University to approve my leave of absence, and shopping expended the rest of my reserves. I love you, but I'm not fond of shopping. Give me scrubs and tennis shoes any day."

Her grandmother raised her hands in defeat. "Fine." She helped Claire go through all the shopping bags and neatly fold the new clothes into piles.

After packing her clothes, computer, books, and everything else she could think of, Claire zipped the final suitcase shut and sank onto the edge of the bed. She sighed. "I guess that's it. We should get some rest. After I spoke to the queen mother letting her know we planned to come, the head of the household, Albert, called me. He said the car would arrive tomorrow around seven a.m. I'm not sure why it's coming so early, but that's the plan."

Granny plopped down beside her and groaned. "Oh, bed sounds good—these old bones ache. You've worn me out."

The two Thomson women readied themselves for bed, turned off the lights, and said goodnight.

Before drifting off to sleep, one thought circled Claire's mind—tomorrow, she would start Royal Lessons. Her chest tightened, but she pushed her worry away. Maybe it wouldn't be so bad. Maybe.

Chapter 6
March 19

Ethan couldn't believe his father expected him to attend a glorified tea party. After returning from his riding debacle with Richard, he found a note card placed on the entryway sideboard. The embossed lettering caught his attention. He picked it up and opened it. It held a letter from the queen mother of Amorley inviting his father and a guest to have tea at her house and meet her long-lost granddaughter and heir to the Crown.

"You're going to this function for me. I have important business meetings, and we cannot turn down the invitation," his father blasted when Ethan protested the event.

Ethan frowned. "Fine, I'll go, but I'm going alone."

"You'll do no such thing—this provides the perfect opportunity to take Lady Abigail."

"Father, I'll go to the castle, but I am not taking Abigail with me. I love you and mother, but if I take her, she'll get the wrong idea."

"She's going to become your wife, Ethan, and the sooner you accept it, the better." His father strode away, the thud of his footsteps across the floor sounded angry and disappointed.

Ethan vowed never to marry Abigail. He didn't care about her fortune or her father's title of head of parliament. None of that mattered to him. Ethan wanted more. He would either remain a bachelor his entire life or marry for love.

Picking up his coat, Ethan walked to the door when Richard stopped him. "Hey, big brother, off to the high tea?" He smirked.

Ethan tried to leave without starting an argument. "Yes, and I need to leave now, or I'm going to arrive late."

Richard gestured with a flourish to let Ethan pass but added one final jab, "It's a shame you won't see that pretty doctor again who saved your ankle. What was her name?"

"Claire. Dr. Claire Thomson. Also, who says I'll never see her again?"

His brother shook his head. "Well, now that Father expects you to take your place in line as the Kane heir, you'll marry Abigail. There'd be no reason to see the doctor. Plus, Father would never allow you to have a relationship with her. She's a commoner."

"I don't care about a person's wealth or status or any of that, and you know it." He glared at Richard.

Richard crossed his arms in front of his chest. "Yeah, but Father cares about it—a lot. I bet if you refused to marry Abigail and took off with a commoner, he'd disown you. Probably take away your inheritance. Of course, then I'd have to step forward as the next in line and help him run things. On second thought, maybe you should pursue the physician."

Ethan's jaw clenched. "I have to go. We can discuss the merits of marrying for love or money later. Father would not disown me."

"We shall see," Richard uttered as he sauntered away.

Putting both conversations with his family out of his mind, Ethan opened the door. The first rays of spring sunshine hit his face. Closing the door behind him, he took a deep breath.

Ethan walked down the stone steps of the Kane estate to the driver and car waiting below. The driver held the door open for him, and he slid in. Richard had made one good point; the kind, beautiful doctor hadn't left his thoughts since he'd met her, and his father would not be happy about that fact.

~

As the car pulled into the stately driveway, Claire's pulse quickened. *Can I do this?* She didn't have time to mull over the question because as soon as the car came to a stop, Granny flung open the door.

The driver had exited and stood by the door with a baffled expression on his face. He likely had never encountered anyone like Margaret Thompson—not many people had.

"Young man, get out of my way. I can manage myself. If you want to be helpful, grab that load of luggage in the trunk." She gestured with her thumb to the rear of the car.

Claire covered her mouth with her hand, stifling a giggle. She slipped out of the car with as much grace as she could muster and smoothed out the outfit she'd chosen for the occasion. Her blue dress seemed too bold in the store, but her grandmother insisted it looked perfect. She recalled her insistence that she wear it for the tea.

"Now that's the one. That's what you have to wear when you meet these fancy people. Plus, didn't you say royal blue covered the walls of that place? I guess they like to do everything royal. You'll match the interior like a mascot."

Claire responded, "I don't think that mascot is quite what I'm going for here. I want my outfit to say I'm taking this seriously, and I'm a respectable person. We both know I'm not good enough for these people. Plus, I'm sure my stepmother, the queen, will be there."

Granny waved away her concern. "Oh, pshaw, who cares about Maurelle. Besides, she's not even a real queen. She married into the family. Now you're in line for the throne. You have an inheritance. Don't forget it."

As Claire considered these words, Milo bounded out of the limousine. He nearly knocked over Albert, who'd come alongside her and placed his hand on her forearm. Milo jumped on Albert and left two muddy pawprints on the front of Albert's white dress shirt underneath his black jacket.

Claire grabbed ahold of Milo's collar and pulled him off the butler. "Albert, I'm so sorry. He doesn't have the best manners but has tons of love to give." She told Milo to sit, and he obliged, his tongue hanging out, panting. She ruffled behind his ears, and his tail wagged.

Albert tried to dust off his shirt. "Oh. Does he belong to you?"

"Yes, this is Milo. The one constant man in my life." She grinned.

Albert gave her a slight frown. "Does the queen mother know about his...presence at the castle?"

Glancing at her best furry friend, Claire bit her lower lip. *What if the castle doesn't allow animals?* That would solve her dilemma because she wouldn't leave Milo for a month. "Well, I didn't tell her about him because our conversation ran brief, but he's a sweetheart and no trouble, I promise." She reached inside her purse and pulled out his blue and gold plaid leash—the one she'd searched for on her shopping trip with her grandmother—and thought it provided a nice touch. Now, Milo matched the castle colors, too.

Staring at the canine, Albert cleared this throat and then shifted his gaze to Claire. He sent her a small smile. "I don't know what she'll say, but he's here, so I suppose we proceed. Perhaps, try to keep him from branding anyone else."

She lifted her forehead, confused. "Branding?"

Pointing at the muddy prints on his shirt, Albert chuckled.

Blood rushed to her cheeks. "Of course."

"Oh, one other thing…the queen, your stepmother, she's…well, she's allergic to dogs. She won't like Sir Milo staying here at all, but I can't say I'm disappointed." He snickered. "I'm glad to see you again. Are you ready?" He raised a brow.

Claire pushed her shoulders back and tightened her grip on Milo's leash. "Yes, I think so."

Albert nodded. "Wonderful. I'll tell Edward to retrieve your luggage and make sure they arrive in both of your rooms."

Claire raised her eyebrows. "Both of our rooms? We're not staying in the same one?"

Albert shook his head. "The castle boasts over a thousand rooms. We've arranged for you each to have your own bedroom in the West Wing. I think you'll approve. Now, come along. The queen mother awaits your arrival in the Grand Banquet Room."

Claire followed Albert to the front entrance, but she paused at the top before walking through the doorway. She called to the butler, "Albert, will the queen be at the tea?"

He stopped and turned, facing Claire and her grandmother. His brows dipped down, and he replied, "Ma'am, I told you she's waiting for you in the Grand Banquet Room."

"No, not the queen mother, Albert. I meant the queen. My stepmother, Maurelle."

A look of understanding flashed across Albert's face. "Oh, I see. Yes, unfortunately, you will have the pleasure of joining both the queen and the queen mother. The queen mother has invited a few members of parliament as well as some other important people to meet you. Don't worry. I'm sure you'll do well. If I may offer one suggestion—"

Claire tilted her head. "Yes, of course, anything."

"Don't try to curtsy again." Albert paused before dispensing further advice, "Simply smile, dip your head, and give a slight bow. Otherwise, you'll do fine."

He looked hesitant about his reassurance, but she murmured, "Thank you, Albert," and followed him down the hallway. He led Claire and Granny into the Grand Banquet Room and stopped. "May I present, Dr. Claire Thomson and her grandmother, Mrs. Margaret Thomson." He bent at the waist.

As he straightened, the queen mother's eyes widened. "Albert, may I inquire what happened to your shirt?"

His cheeks turned a rose color, and his eyes darted to Claire. He sent her a conspiratorial smile. "Yes, ma'am. I received a warm welcome from our third houseguest for the month." He gestured to the pooch who had loped into the room, bringing up the rear of the procession. "Mr. Milo Thomson, the golden retriever. A spirited yet loving fellow."

The table had filled except for three empty seats. Claire took her place with the queen mother on one side and Granny Margaret on the other while Albert spoke. Albert turned and left the room as if this piece of information were ordinary.

The queen mother shifted her attention to her granddaughter, and her brow lifted higher. "Am I to understand that you've brought a dog to the castle?"

"Um…yes, ma'am. I hope it's okay. He's part of my family. I couldn't leave him behind for a month." Claire dipped her head in a seated version of a curtsy and thanked the attendant who'd helped tuck in her seat as she took her place.

"I suppose it will be fine. I'll tell Albert to make appropriate accommodations for Sir Milo." The queen mother sat at the head of the long, cherry table housing twenty golden finished chairs in the Grand Banquet Room. At one end of the room sat a matching sideboard topped with a blue and white china vase bigger than Claire, and the other wall boasted several pieces of artwork. One massive window above the sideboard allowed glorious rays of sunlight to flood the room.

Claire's stepmother, Queen Maurelle, entered the room, and her eyes landed upon Milo. She made a distinct clicking sound with her tongue and took her seat. "I guess no one recalls my intense—" she emphasized the word intense, "—allergies to dogs. I cough and sneeze, and oh, I despise the creatures. They're awful."

Claire sipped her cup of tea. She found keeping her hands busy and her mouth full left little time to pick up the wrong spoon or say something ridiculous.

Queen Maurelle locked her eyes on Claire. "Now, my dear, am I to understand that you practice the art of—what did your grandmother call it? Orthopedic surgery?"

Claire placed her teacup on its saucer and lifted her eyes to meet Maurelle's. "Yes, that's correct, though it's more of a science than an art."

Peering over her china cup, Maurelle narrowed her eyes. "How is it possible for you to be here for a month as a practicing surgeon? Won't you be missed? Moreover, how do you plan to take the Throne and run a country while doing surgery?" She took a long draw of her tea before placing it on the saucer with a clink.

Maurelle had stated many of the concerns on Claire's mind. She didn't know how she'd do it all. Maybe it wouldn't be possible. Still, she had to try. "I spoke with my program director at Oxmund University before coming here, and he approved my leave. I'm already a board-certified orthopedic surgeon, but I took the fellowship to improve my skill set and pursue a particular area of interest. Regarding how I'd run a country or be the queen and a surgeon at the same time—well, I don't know, but—"

At that moment, the handsome horseback riding, tea-drinking, ankle-twisting man she'd tended to by the roadside strolled through the doors. His eyes landed upon Claire and lit up with recognition. He smiled.

"Hello. What are you doing here?"

The queen mother turned toward him and waved him over with a flick of her hand. "Ethan, come here and meet my granddaughter, Claire. She's a surgeon and, from what I've heard, an excellent one. Claire has agreed to spend the next month with me and learn about what it takes to be a Royal. I'm hoping at the month's end she'll feel prepared to take her rightful place as the future queen of Amorley."

Ethan's face paled, and his smile faded a bit. He wore black dress pants and a blazer with a pressed white shirt underneath. His attire looked similar to Albert's. Stepping closer to the table, he addressed Claire, "Queen of Amorley?" He waited for her confirmation.

Nervous, Claire twirled a strand of her hair with one finger. "Nothing's been decided. I only wanted to learn more about my—"

Granny cut in, "Hey, handsome, do you mind getting me some more of that chai tea? I like things hot and spicy." She winked at him and returned her attention to the third scone she'd partaken of for the day.

Snapping her head toward Granny, Claire sent her a warning look and gasped. "I can't believe you said that." With a flick of her eyes to Ethan again, she gulped. "I'm so sorry. My grandmother doesn't mean anything by it. She flirts with everyone. It's her way."

Ethan scrunched his forehead, his face now three shades past crimson. "It's okay. I thought the queen mother was your grandmother."

Dabbing her lips with a napkin, the queen mother gestured toward Granny. "Where are my manners?

Ethan, let me introduce Mrs. Margaret Thomson of Boston, Massachusetts. She is Claire's other grandmother. She'll be staying with me for the month as well. Oh, and the dog." She tipped her head toward Milo seated on the floor next to Claire.

Claire's stepmother made a sound of disapproval at the mention of the canine.

The queen mother spoke, changing the subject, "May I ask a favor of you, Ethan?"

He leaned down. "Anything, ma'am," he replied, not taking his eyes off Claire.

"Would you tell Albert the tea has turned cold and teatime has ended? I'm sorry to cut the welcome short, but my granddaughter must want to settle into her room. I'm sure you have other tasks to tend to as well." The queen mother rose from her seat.

All nineteen of the other guests followed suit and stood.

Did Ethan work for the castle? He certainly looked the part. Ethan hadn't told her about his occupation when she had met him.

Ethan bowed. "Of course, ma'am. I'll tell him."

The queen mother stepped away from the table, her straight royal blue skirt still wrinkle-free, and left the room. Everyone else at the gathering followed her, and soon only Claire, Granny, and Ethan remained. Claire circled the table to the other side next to Ethan. She caught his gaze. "I can't believe you're here. It seems like you're everywhere lately."

He sent her a warm smile. "I know, but I'm glad."

Heat rose from Claire's chest and filled her cheeks. "Thanks, me too. If you don't have to leave soon, perhaps we could take a walk around the—"

The queen mother called from the hallway. "Claire? Claire, dear. Hurry along. I have many things to show you, and you still need to unpack."

Claire sighed and shrugged. "Guess I have to go. I hope to see you again soon."

Ethan grinned and gave her a wave. "Me, too."

Claire walked out of the room, Granny in tow. As they entered the hallway, Granny mumbled, "Looks like that hunk of a man has eyes for you."

Whipping her head around, she hissed, "Behave! Besides, who knows if I'll see him in the future. For all we know, he works for the queen mother. He's probably off-limits."

Her granny rolled her eyes. "Pshaw. Off-limits. I'd say once you're the queen of Amorley, you can set the limits yourself and probably have your pick of gentlemen callers."

Shaking her head, Claire turned and pasted a smile on her face, ready to address her royal grandmother while trying to quash Granny's words out of her mind.

A thin voice whispered from behind, "Pick of them…"

Claire heaved another sigh and tucked a loose tendril behind her ear. Granny would never change. She followed the queen mother down the hallway and up a circular staircase toward the West Wing.

The queen mother glanced over her shoulder and smiled. "Get some rest. I'll take you on a short tour later this evening and tomorrow we will begin Royal Lessons."

Yep. That's what Claire feared—would she be prepared? Would she be good enough? She'd find out tomorrow.

ROYALLY CONFUSED

Chapter 7
March 20

Claire wore one size too small black pantyhose, a royal blue pencil skirt that allowed little room to maneuver much less walk, and a white button-up shirt so starched she thought she could break it like a cracker. Walking into the drawing room, Claire noted an empty seat next to the queen mother.

Her grandmother waved her over, and Claire took careful, short steps. Claire suspected she looked like a motorized wind-up toy trying to cross the room in her skirt. *Why did fancy clothing have to feel so uncomfortable?* She'd never missed her sneakers and scrubs so much.

Sinking onto the blue and gold silk-tufted cushion, Claire attempted to cross one leg over the other unsuccessfully.

Her grandmother pursed her lips and gave a slight shake of her head. "No, dear. First Royal Lesson for the day—a lady crosses her feet at the ankle and keeps her knees together. Like this." She gestured to her pose on her chair. "Now show me."

Claire stared at her grandmother for a moment, taking in her grace and poise. She made moving in the straitjacket of a skirt seem simple, and her grandmother's skirt looked even tighter and longer than Claire's. Pulling in a deep breath, Claire muttered, "Okay." She used her hands to lift the top knee off the other one and, with both legs on the ground, crossed them at the ankle. Unsure of where to place her hands, she decided at the last minute to let them hang at her sides.

Watching her granddaughter's stilted movements, the queen mother sent Claire a half-smile. "Better. Don't let your arms hang down like a monkey. Put them on your lap, one hand on top of the other."

Claire's hands flew to her lap.

The queen mother rewarded Claire with her first full smile of the day. "Good. Now, you look like a lady. It's important to maintain this position any time you sit in a chair, at a table, or ride in a car."

"Got it," Claire confirmed.

Her grandmother lifted her glasses, scooting them higher up her nose. "Now, onto lesson two: walking."

Claire scrunched her forehead. "How hard can walking be? I walk everywhere every day."

The queen mother peered at her granddaughter over the brim of her glasses as if debating this point. "Show me. Let me see you walk to the window, turn around, and come back."

Claire rose from her seat. *Should she keep her hands folded in front of her while she walked? Should her hands remain glued together at all times? Surely not.* She shook her hands out and cracked her neck to the right side, then the left. Taking short, quick steps to the window, Claire stared at the ground to avoid tripping on something. When she arrived at the window, she pivoted like a runway model and then resumed her six-inch-long steps back to her grandmother. "How's that?"

"Hmm, well, you walked. However, it's not quite what we're going for here. Let's try it again. Follow me." Her grandmother rose and walked toward the window.

Claire watched her grandmother and fell in line behind her.

"Now, see how I take long strides? You don't want to look like a puppy tugging against the leash. Let your arms swing by your sides. Counter body movement. Don't overthink it."

As they both arrived at the window, Claire interrupted her grandmother's lecture, "Ma'am, I thought you told me not to let my arms hang at my sides—the monkey thing, remember?"

Pivoting much slower and smoother than Claire had on her first walking effort, the queen mother met Claire's gaze. "Yes, that's true, but the key differences here are to keep your shoulders back, your neck long, and your head lifted. Let your shoulders carry your arms, don't let them sag, and—" the queen mother placed her hand under Claire's chin, lifting her head, "don't stare at your feet. Ever. Especially if you're walking. Trust your feet—you won't fall."

Claire snorted. "You don't know that. I don't trust my feet—at least not in three-inch black patent heels."

"Don't snort," her grandmother clucked.

Smiling, Claire nodded her understanding. "Right. No snorting."

The queen mother walked away, returning to her seat.

Claire realized her grandmother expected her to do

the same. She did her head-lifted, shoulder-straightened, regal walk back to her grandmother. When she sank into her chair, she released the breath she'd been holding.

A wide grin spread across her grandmother's face, and she said, "Good. An improvement."

Claire's shoulders started to relax, and then she yanked them back and straightened her posture. "Thanks."

The queen mother rang a bell on the small table next to her chair.

Within seconds, Albert appeared. "Ma'am, how may I help you?"

Removing her glasses, she let them hang around her neck on the golden chain attached to them. "Yes, Albert, we will take our meal now, please."

He gave a slight bow, wearing his usual uniform of black slacks pressed with the line down the front and a black suit jacket. "Yes, of course. Would you like me to help you to the Grand Banquet Room?"

Her grandmother shook her head. "No, thank you. We can manage. Claire and I will make our way there."

Albert retreated, leaving them alone again.

She rose and looked down at her granddaughter. "Ready, my dear?"

Bolting up from her chair, Claire answered, "Yes, ma'am, of course." She followed her grandmother into the Grand Banquet Room, taking her seat on the table's opposite side.

At the periphery of the room stood three waitstaff in formal attire, while at the corner of the room near the door connecting to the kitchen, stood Albert. He sent Claire a nearly imperceptible wink of encouragement.

Claire flashed him a nervous grin and then gazed at the table setting. In front of her sat a larger white plate underneath a smaller royal blue plate decorated with the blue and gold Amorley crest. It looked expensive. *Don't break it.* To the upper right corner of the place setting were two glasses, and in the left corner sat a smaller white plate with a knife laid across the middle of it. A tiny fork and spoon rested above the plate, and two more forks, two spoons, and one knife resided on the left and right sides of the big plate.

"Wow. That's a lot of utensils." At home, Claire would consider herself fortunate to have one of each clean at any given time.

"Yes, I wanted to start our next lesson—Table Manners. Any royal person needs impeccable table manners and to know how to set a table. Hence, our practice meal today."

A wave of excitement rushed through Claire. Eating—finally a lesson she could handle. She felt bad that she'd left her granny alone in her room, though. Claire hadn't wanted to wake her this morning. "Um, ma'am?"

"Yes?" Her grandmother lifted her eyes to meet Claire's.

Claire's stomach growled. She glanced at the watch on her wrist. *Noon.* "I wonder if I should check on Granny. I didn't talk with her this morning, and I don't know if she made her way to breakfast."

As if on cue, her granny strolled into the Grand Banquet Room. "Good afternoon, everyone. Isn't it a glorious day?"

Claire's mouth dropped open. Granny wore a royal blue top and matching pants and a gold hat twice the size of her head with a blue feather sticking out the top of it. As she approached the dining table, the feather waved with each step. Clamping her mouth shut and trying to stifle a giggle, Claire snickered. After a few seconds, she broke the silence, "Granny, what have you been doing?"

Granny sat down in the chair next to Claire, ignoring the fact that only two place settings lay on the table. "Oh, a little of this and that. Albert showed me to the parlor and brought me some toast and tea, and then I fed Milo and took him for a walk through the gardens. He loved it—even found a bird and brought it back to old queenie. She didn't seem impressed."

Claire arched a brow. "Queenie?"

"Old Queenie Maurelle." She leaned closer to the table, lowering her voice in a conspiratorial whisper, "You know, she doesn't like Milo. Maybe not me, either—not that it bothers me."

As if she'd heard her name spoken, Claire's stepmother, the queen, entered the room. "Well, what do we have here?"

Claire's heart ticked up, and she swallowed hard before answering, "Um, I'm doing Royal Lessons. The queen mother wanted to teach me table manners."

Maurelle wore a look of disdain. "I see. How sweet. Claire, I wonder if I might ask a favor of you?"

Rubbing her sweaty palms against her skirt under the table so nobody could see, Claire gave a cautious reply, "What is it?"

The queen inspected her blood-red fingernails, refusing to meet Claire's eyes as she spoke, "Please keep your mutt and the wild game he finds away from me. As you know, I have allergies—and standards."

Anger bubbled in Claire's chest and threatened to spew out of her mouth, but she recalled her Sunday school lessons on taming her tongue. Taking a breath, Claire responded, "I'll do my best to keep him out of your way, but as to the things he catches—Milo doesn't mean any harm. He loves chasing birds and retrieving things. His DNA dictates it. I'm not sure that anyone can eliminate that drive. I'm sorry he bothered you." *What a difficult woman.*

Her stepmother rose from the table and studied Claire, a menacing gleam in her eyes. "See that you do. Enjoy your lunch. I'm sure you'll need all the practice you can get. You'll discover it's more difficult being royal than you might think."

After Queen Maurelle left the room, Claire shuddered. "Wow. She hates me."

The queen mother tried to ease her granddaughter's concerns. "No, dear, it's not you per se. She wants the Crown for herself—well, for your half-brother, Eric. You haven't met him yet because he's away at university. He's next in line for the throne if you cannot or will not accept the title and its obligations. She'd love to have him at the helm so she can run things from behind the scenes."

Claire smoothed her hair and tucked the front strands behind each ear.

Her grandmother continued, "I refuse to let that happen. Maurelle longs for ultimate power and has little concern for Amorley or its people. I believe she married your father so that one day she would rule. With his passing and me finding you, she feels threatened—as she should. Ignore Maurelle. Leave her to me."

Claire remained silent and nodded.

Albert and the waitstaff began placing course after course on the table. With each selection, the queen mother advised Claire and Granny which utensil to use. When the meal ended, Claire had made half a dozen mistakes but didn't injure herself or anyone else, so she considered it a win. That's when she lifted the bowl filled with water next to her and took a long sip.

The queen mother's hand flew to cover her mouth.

Granny laughed.

Claire returned it to the table and frowned. "What did I do this time?"

The queen mother placed her hand on top of Claire's across the table. "My dear, that's the finger bowl. You clean your fingertips in it."

Claire felt her face flush. "I'm so sorry. I didn't know."

"It's fine. You'll learn. Now, for my last lesson of the day."

Dread filled Claire's stomach and caused it to churn. *No more. Please.* "Okay, what is it?"

Her grandmother sent her a kind smile. "Would you like to come with me to the study and learn more about your father? I have several picture albums I think you'd enjoy, and I'd love to show them to you—if you feel ready."

"Yes, please. I'd love that." Turning to Granny, Claire asked, "Do you want to come with us?"

Understanding flashed across her granny's face, and she squeezed Claire's shoulder before standing. "No, I think I'll see if I can find a few more ways to pester that queenie. Maybe Milo will bring her a rat next time or a ground squirrel. Do they have ground squirrels here?"

The queen mother didn't respond in words but made

a displeased noise.

Claire stood and gave Granny a quick hug, whispering in her ear, "I don't think I'd mention the dog's antics anymore. Try to keep him away from the local wildlife." She stepped back and grinned, feeling like maybe she was starting to get the hang of this royal thing.

Granny winked. "Deal." Then, she hurried out of the room.

The queen mother rose from her seat and walked toward the Great Hall.

Claire took her cue and stood, following her grandmother down the hall and into the study.

Her grandmother took her place behind an old, mahogany writing desk and pointed to an open chair next to her.

Claire sat in the chair beside her and pored over stacks of picture albums of her father's life. "I can't believe how much I look like him," she marveled. He had her blue eyes, but his hair appeared to be a few shades darker, almost light brown.

Grandmother pointed to another photo. "The royal historian took this picture on his Coronation Day—one of the happiest days of my life. Look at your grandfather and me in the background. He courted me for six months and won my heart. When he proposed, I didn't hesitate with my answer." She ran her finger over the picture and wore a wistful smile. "We shared many wonderful years. I miss him terribly."

Claire smiled at her grandmother. "It must have been amazing to have someone know you so well—to go through all of life's experiences together. Sometimes, I don't think I'll ever have that. Well, except for my relationship with Granny." She chuckled.

The queen mother turned to face Claire. "You will. I know you will." She closed the photo album. "I want you to know how much your father would have loved you, cherished you. Your father and stepmother tried to have a child for many years after they married before finally celebrating the joyful news of your half-brother's birth. I've never seen him so happy as the day he found out he would become a father. If he'd learned about you, he'd have loved and cherished you as well. Maybe even more because of how intensely he felt about your mother."

A single tear rolled down Claire's cheek. She brushed it away with her fingertip and dried it on her lap. "Thank you. I've always thought something was wrong with me—some reason that my father would leave my mother and me and never look back. As a teenager, part of me longed for him to walk through the door and scoop me into his arms. The rest of me despised him for abandoning us, and I never wanted to meet him. I know God calls us to love everyone, but if my father didn't love me, why should I love him? I thought I must not be worth anything for him to discard me so easily." A small sob escaped her lips, and more tears fell.

In an uncharacteristic show of emotion, the queen mother leaned in and wrapped her arms around her granddaughter. She patted her on the back. "There, there, dear. You are valued. You are important. When I received your call, I couldn't believe it. Come to think of it, that was the best day of my life. To learn another piece of my son lived on inside another person, inside of you—it thrilled me." She leaned back and looked at her granddaughter's face, then smiled and shifted into Queen Mother, Giver of Royal Lessons mode, and continued, "Now, dry those tears. We have a lot on our agenda tomorrow. It's the National Polo Charity, and we provide the opening remarks. Do you know how to ride?" She lifted her brow.

Claire pushed at the remaining tears with the back of her hand before answering, "Um…a horse?"

Her grandmother gave a slight nod. "Yes, a horse."

"No, but how hard can it be? I don't have to jump over obstacles or do anything crazy, right?"

Her grandmother rose from her seat and stacked the photo albums on top of the desk. She peered down at Claire. "No, you don't have to jump over any obstacles. We will promenade around the field and end at the center. I usually make a brief announcement, but I thought you might say a few words. I'm sure the country wants to hear from their potential future queen."

Claire's throat tightened. She swallowed hard. "Riding on top of a horse and then public speaking."

"Yes, will that be a problem?" the queen mother asked.

Staring at the stack of albums, Claire wished she could rewind to the few seconds prior when they'd bonded over photographs. She loathed public speaking. Sure, her academic medicine role might require her to give the occasional lecture, but Claire lived and breathed medicine. As long as she had a prepared slideshow and her notes, she could muscle through that endeavor. Speaking to a crowd as the possible future queen of Amorley… A wave of nausea washed over her, and a bitter taste stung her mouth. "I don't know if

I can do it."

"Of course, you can. You will say hello to the crowd and welcome them on behalf of the royal family. Then, we'll dismount and walk to our box seats and watch the match." She grinned and tilted her head toward Claire. "I think you'll enjoy the polo match. It's one of the country's favorite pastimes, and I've always loved it myself." She gave a nod, settling the matter. "You'll do fine."

Claire gazed after her grandmother as she left the study. Tomorrow, she had to ride on a horse, which she'd never done in her life, and give a speech to the entire country from atop the horse. Her grandmother's words echoed in her thoughts, "You'll do fine." *Yeah, right.*

~

Ethan hadn't stopped thinking about Claire since the tea the other day. Aside from admiring her beauty, he saw goodness in her eyes and smile. Her blonde hair shone when the sunlight hit it through the large window in the Grand Banquet Room, and her blue eyes flashed intelligence and kindness. Remembering the contours of her face made his pulse quicken, and he hoped he'd see her at the upcoming polo charity event.

The Kane family boasted a long history of equestrians, and polo came with the territory. Since the age of five, he'd been riding horses, and his father made it clear that his two sons would represent the family at the event tomorrow.

"Ethan," his father barked, "are you listening to me?" His face softened as Ethan's mother leaned over and planted a kiss on her husband's cheek, trying to ease the tension. He squeezed her hand. After the brief reprieve his mother's interruption provided, Ethan's father resumed interrogating his son. "This is important. Did you hear a word of what I said?"

Turning to meet his father's gaze, Ethan pushed away the thoughts of Dr. Claire Thomson. "I did."

Ethan's father matched his eldest son's height of six foot two and had the same rugged good looks. He wore his blond hair cut shorter than Ethan's, but his blue eyes often held disdain or contempt. With a strong jaw and fit physique, he could pass as Ethan's older brother. "Then what did I say?"

Ethan circled his spoon in his tea, tapped the edge of the cup, and placed the utensil on the saucer. He lifted the cup to his lips and took a long drink before setting it down and responding, "You said the National Polo Charity event is tomorrow. I heard."

His father narrowed his eyes and leaned closer. "I expect you and your brother to put on a good showing. Abigail and her family will attend, and I want to have a conversation with her father and you. We have a lot of details to discuss if you two are to wed within the next year."

Ethan's mother sat to the right of her husband at the long dining table. She had a short, light blonde bob and blue eyes. At five foot one, she always stood at her husband's chest level. Placing a hand on her husband's arm, Louise Kane attempted to calm her husband and smooth relations between him and her firstborn. She spoke in a soft voice, "Now, dear, must we entertain such talk at the dinner hour?"

Her husband maintained an unwavering gaze at his son. "I think now provides the perfect opportunity to discuss this matter. Ethan, I told you the other day that it's settled. You will marry Abigail."

Anger rose in Ethan's chest, but he forced his voice to remain calm. "Respectfully, Father, I told you that I'm not marrying her. I don't care that her father holds rank as the head of parliament and can pave the way for future land deals for you. It also doesn't matter that Abigail's family has more money than the Crown. None of that is important to me."

His father slammed his fist on the table.

Ethan's mother pulled her hand back and placed it on her chest.

Ethan suspected she didn't care who he married, but she'd never go against her husband's wishes.

Lifting a finger to Ethan's face, his father spat out his following words, "Now see here. You will participate in the polo match tomorrow. You will ride well. You will talk with Abigail and her father about your and Abigail's future, and you will do all of this with a smile on your face because I am your father and head of this estate and family. I don't want to hear anything further on this matter." Ethan's father rose from the table and stormed out of the room.

Scooting one seat closer to her son, Ethan's mother put a gentle hand on his shoulder. "Ethan...I know he seems harsh, but he only wants the best for the family. He believes Abigail and her family are the best for you."

Shaking his head, Ethan wondered how Richard always escaped these heartwarming meals with the excuse of long hours at work. "No, Mother. He wants the most money and power for this family. He doesn't care about my wishes or what's best for me." Rising from the table, Ethan threw his napkin on top of his plate and followed his father's lead, vacating the dining room.

He didn't want to disrespect his parents, but he couldn't marry someone he didn't love, and Ethan didn't love Abigail Fulton. He didn't know if he even tolerated her. Either way, he'd stall for time and attend the polo match tomorrow. Perhaps, he'd find a way to convince his father to see his side of things. If nothing else, Ethan knew the royal family attended the polo charity event each year, so Ethan prayed he'd see Claire again, too. At least she'd provide a ray of sunlight through the darkness of his family obligations.

Chapter 8
March 21

Claire stared at herself in her bedroom floor-length mirror and scrunched her nose. She looked ridiculous. The queen mother had insisted Claire wear traditional Amorley riding attire. Black riding pants so tight they cut off the circulation to her lower half covered Claire's legs. She wore a fitted white button-up shirt and a royal blue blazer with the Amorley crest on the left breast. Across her chest at a diagonal lay a golden sash, indicating her royal affiliation—as if she needed any further proof in this outfit. A riding hat completed the ensemble. It had a chin pad that dug into her face and a strap that choked her neck—a far difference from her scrubs.

A knock on the door interrupted her inspection in the mirror. Claire called, "Come in."

Granny opened the door and stuck her head through the doorway. "Are you ready? I think old Albie said the queen mother started pacing downstairs about five minutes ago. I never pegged her as a pacer, but people surprise you."

After one last glimpse at her reflection, Claire decided she couldn't improve upon the outfit. She closed her eyes and said a quick, silent prayer she wouldn't fall off the horse, forget her speech, or otherwise embarrass herself or the royal family. Opening her eyes, she tried to bend her legs in the pants and give them one final stretch but to no avail. "I'm ready. I can't breathe or move, but I'm ready."

Her granny stared at the outfit and snickered. "Oh, now I've seen everything. Let's go. If we don't get downstairs soon, they may stuff us in the second car with the evil queenie. My indigestion already flared today. A car ride with Maurelle—" Her grandmother pursed her lips. She mimicked Claire's stepmother's snobbish tone, "—might send me to the hospital." She rubbed her chest for emphasis.

"Hmm, you have a point. Let's hurry." Claire followed Granny out of the bedroom and turned off the light on the way out.

The two Thomson women made it downstairs and into an awaiting black limousine devoid of Queen Maurelle. They rode along in silence with the queen mother and one of her assistants.

Almost thirty minutes later, Claire looked out the window and saw the polo field and stadium entrance. A wrought-iron archway greeted them, and the entire periphery boasted green bushes and bluish-purple and yellow fragrant flowers.

The limousine rolled to a stop in front of a smaller seating area. It appeared to hold twenty or so people. A white tent protected the space overhead, and "reserve" signs hanging from ropes lined the aisles.

The queen mother pointed to the reserved zone. "Those are our seats. It's the Royal Box. After we greet the participants and do the Royal Promenade across the front of the field, you'll give your speech over there."

She indicated to another set of bleachers able to accommodate several hundred people with a white tent overhead. "That's the main stadium seating for all of the visitors."

The queen mother's door opened, and she and her assistant slid out. Claire and her granny followed suit, and as Claire stood, the buckle under her chin seemed to tighten. She swallowed hard. "Those horses look big, and the field is huge—larger than a football field." She tugged at her chin strap, wondering if she could still bail.

Not picking up on her granddaughter's nerves, the queen mother nodded and began a lesson on the intricacies of polo. "The field is three-hundred yards, and the opposite end of the field houses the stables and horses. Each rider participates on a thoroughbred. The horse wears an English-style saddle and has its mane clipped short and its tail braided to avoid interference with the game. Four riders represent each team, with their goal to hit a plastic ball with a wooden mallet between the goal post."

Claire nodded. "Seems straightforward."

Agreeing, the queen mother waved for Claire to follow her as they talked. " It can get aggressive. The riders may hit one another's mallets and ride alongside an opponent to push them out of the way. It's quite exciting at times. You'll love it."

I'm sure—if Claire didn't die before the match started either by getting thrown off her horse or from stage fright. "Um, ma'am, I'm still not convinced it's a great idea for me to give the welcoming remarks. I told you I'm not the best public speaker. Give me a scalpel and a broken bone, and I'm fantastic, but put me behind a microphone—I don't know—I might faint."

The queen mother shook her head. "You'll manage. You have to if you're to take the Throne, and believe me, I want nothing more than that. I cannot bear the idea of the alternative." She shivered. "Now, join me at the stable. We have to mount up and prepare because the match will start soon."

Claire glanced to her left and noted several people lined up beyond the gate, ready to enter the stadium. She pulled in a breath and released it slowly before walking behind the queen mother to meet her horse.

Twenty minutes later, Claire stood next to her saddled horse. She placed her hands on the saddle for a second before withdrawing them. Staring at the animal, Claire wondered if she could trust him.

The queen mother urged her on, "Grab the saddle firmly, place one foot in the stirrup, and then on the count of three, swing the other leg up and over the back of the horse. It's easy."

Claire nodded. She placed her right foot in the saddle and counted aloud, "1, 2, 3." Then, she swung her left leg over and landed with her backside on the saddle. A wide grin erupted for a second before Claire realized she faced the tail end of the horse. "Uh, ma'am, I don't think it worked."

The queen mother guided her horse alongside Claire's and frowned. "Oh, dear. No, that won't do. Swing your left leg back off while holding the saddle and ease yourself to the ground. You'll have to try again."

Claire obeyed her grandmother's instructions and caught herself at the last minute before she planted her bottom on the muddy ground below.

"Now, put your left foot in the stirrup. The right leg should swing over. Then, you'll face the correct direction. Very important." Her grandmother stared, waiting for Claire to right herself.

Gripping the saddle once more, Claire prayed for God to help her land correctly this time. "Okay, here I go." She heaved herself up again and this time landed facing the horse's head. "I did it."

Her grandmother nodded. "You did. Now, we must hurry. I want to welcome the riders, and then it's time for the Royal Promenade. Follow me."

Granny had opted to stay safely on the ground, and Claire couldn't blame her. She sent a teasing grin to Claire as the royal family clip-clopped toward the other end of the stables.

Upon their arrival, eight strapping gentlemen lined up with their hands at their sides, holding their helmets under one arm.

Claire scanned the riders, and her eyes widened when she saw a familiar face. "Ethan, hello." She waved from her saddle.

Ethan didn't seem surprised to see Claire and sent her a smile and a nod.

He must have known the royal family would be here today. Claire hoped it pleased him. She worried everyone could see her heart pounding through her blazer. Allowing her eyes to flit toward Ethan once more, she couldn't deny an attraction to him.

The queen mother stepped her horse forward and spoke, "Good afternoon. Thank you for riding in the National Polo Charity Match today. It's an important event that provides additional funding to our local hospital and underprivileged patients. Today, you will all play a role in bettering Amorley. I want to take a moment and introduce my granddaughter, Dr. Claire Thomson, the potential heir to the Amorley Crown. She'll be riding in the Royal Promenade with me and giving the welcoming remarks."

All eight riders bowed at the waist to acknowledge Claire's presence.

Claire felt her cheeks warm, and she wanted to slide off the horse again.

"Now, I'll pray for an entertaining and safe match today, and then we'll start the event." The queen mother bowed her head and spoke a few short words of prayer and then led the group toward the opposite end of the stable. She turned and glanced over her shoulder. "Claire, are you ready?"

Claire's face still burned, and she found it hard to tear her eyes away from Ethan's, but she shifted her gaze toward her grandmother and nodded. "Yes."

"Good, keep a good grip on your reins. Don't worry. The horse knows what to do. As long as you don't make any sudden movements, he'll do his job." Her grandmother led them closer to the main seating area.

Claire lifted her eyes and noted the stadium had filled while they met with the riders. She swallowed hard. *Don't freak out, and don't panic. Stay calm.* She gripped the reins tighter and prayed the horse would behave.

An overhead intercom called out, "Now we welcome the Amorley royal family with the traditional Polo Promenade to begin the first event of the season."

The queen mother guided her horse along the field's edge in front of the stadium's front row. The horse picked up his feet in a slow trot, his head held high, as if knowing the important figurehead he carried. Her grandmother made it look effortless.

After a few more members of the family led the way, Claire's horse moved forward. She jolted upright. *Elbows in, heels down, head lifted, smile but not too much.* She tried to rehearse in her head all the things the queen mother had said earlier. Claire survived the Promenade with no issues, and the entire crowd rose from their seats and gave polite applause.

As the horses lined up facing the main stadium bleachers, Claire realized sweat completely drenched her shirt. The time had come to give the welcoming remarks.

The announcer walked over to Claire and handed her a microphone.

Claire's hand shook as she took it from him. She looked at its handle to check the power button and asked, "Is this thing on?" Her question reverberated throughout the field and provided the answer. *Great. Super start.* "Uh…um, so I'm Claire…Dr. Claire Thomson and I want to thank you for having me today. This will be my first polo match, so I'm excited to experience this country's great sport. I hope to meet many of you soon and continue to learn more about my father, my family, and this beautiful country and its people. Thanks. I mean, thank you." Then, she tipped her head in a slight bow. *What a disaster.* At least she'd survived it, and now she could relax, get off the horse, and watch the match.

A few people in the crowd clapped, and then others joined in a resounding applause.

Relief and hope washed over Claire. Maybe she

could do this royal thing. Perhaps she could learn to become a queen. Did she even want the position? What about her fellowship? She couldn't imagine never seeing another patient again. Medicine had been her solitary goal her entire life. Still, she wondered—had medicine become a way for her to prove her worth?

Claire's palms dampened, and when the announcer returned by her side ready to retrieve the microphone, Claire let the device slip from her grasp. It fell to the ground and she gasped. It had landed in an unfortunate location atop a pile of...well, another horse's business. Claire's hand flew to her mouth. *This could not be considered a royal thing to do.* Her gaze darted to the queen mother whose face paled.

Granny sat on the front row of the Royal Box. She covered her mouth, snickering. At least one person looked delighted.

Her eyes flicked toward her stepmother. Make that two delighted people. Queen Maurelle barely concealed her grin.

The announcer's eyes widened, but he reassured Claire, "Please, ma'am, do not worry. I'll get it sterilized and ask for another one in the meantime. It's no problem."

Closing her eyes, Claire waited for a reprieve, but when the ground didn't engulf her, she opened them and responded, "Thanks."

After her microphone debacle, Claire couldn't wait to hop off her horse and take her seat. She found her spot in the Royal Box seats and dropped her head into her hands. Thankfully, the game began and provided a much-needed distraction.

She couldn't deny her enjoyment at observing

Ethan's sportsmanship. He and his brother Richard played for the same team and ninety minutes later won the match.

Claire jumped to her feet in an unladylike manner and clapped. As she opened her mouth to give a "Wahoo," her grandmother sent her a shake of the head.

Plopping down in her seat at the match's conclusion, Claire noticed a group of riders huddled in the center of the field.

The announcer's voice sounded over the loudspeaker, "May I ask if we have an available physician to come to center field? It appears we have an injured rider, and the polo match's on-call doctor remains stuck in traffic."

Without any hesitation, Claire's hand shot in the air. She yelled, "I'm a doctor. I'm coming." She ran as fast as her tight pants would carry her to the patient, thankful she'd removed her helmet earlier. Wisps of hair escaped from her tidy low bun at the nape of her neck. She shoved them back to no avail as the wind blew.

Out of breath, Claire arrived at her patient—a rider from the losing team. He wore a red polo shirt, white pants, and a pained expression on his face. He gripped his right elbow with his left hand and groaned.

Claire knelt next to him and gave him a reassuring smile. "Hi, I'm Dr. Thomson. I'm the one who dropped the microphone in…well, you know."

This joke made her patient's face relax a bit.

Claire placed a gentle hand on his unaffected shoulder. "What happened?"

He grimaced. "The last whack I gave the ball did

something to my arm because my elbow hurts, and I can't move it."

She met his gaze. "Mind if I take a look? I'm an orthopedic surgeon."

He nodded. "Sure. Anything to make the pain stop."

Claire examined his arm and asked him to do a few maneuvers before giving her assessment. "Yep, you've dislocated your elbow. Do you want me to fix it?"

He frowned. "Is it going to hurt?"

She scrunched her forehead. "Well, it won't feel good, but if I reduce it, you'll feel a lot better. You'll still need to ice it and rest. What do you say?"

He groaned again before answering, "Do it."

Claire asked him to lie on his chest on a portable stretcher some of the players had retrieved. They lifted him so his right arm hung down. Claire looked at Ethan. "Can you hold his injured hand like this?" She demonstrated the technique to him.

Sending her a small smile, Ethan bowed. "Sure."

"Don't be afraid to apply tension. Otherwise, this won't work," Claire advised.

Ethan caught her gaze. "Tension—not a problem."

Claire's heart raced, but she turned her attention to the patient. "Okay, now, sir, I'm going to apply pressure to your elbow while Ethan pulls downward on your wrist. It may hurt—a lot. Are you ready?"

He grunted, "Ready."

She glanced at Ethan again. "On the count of three—one, two, three." The two of them did their part, and the patient yelped in pain but then relaxed a bit.

The patient turned his head to face Claire. "Thanks, Dr. Thomson. You saved me. I'd be honored to call you my future queen."

Heat rushed up from Claire's chest to her face, and she smiled. "You're welcome. No thanks necessary." She turned to Ethan. "Thanks for your help. You did a great job."

Shaking his head, he grabbed one of her hands. "No, you were amazing. I would love to see you sometime—outside of fancy events and teas. Would you be available to take a walk with me tomorrow? I could come to the castle, and we could walk the gardens."

She glanced toward the stadium housing the royal family and realized she'd made another spectacle of herself. Sending him a warm smile, she nodded. "I'd love that. I don't know what my grandmother has scheduled for Royal Lessons tomorrow, but maybe I can talk her into taking a lunch break. Would noon work?"

Still holding her hand, Ethan agreed, "Yes."

Her fingers tingled, and she hated to pull away from him, but she'd never seen the queen mother look so flabbergasted.

Granny, however, appeared pleased at the afternoon's developments. She wore a head-to-toe royal blue outfit again, but this time she'd added matching gloves. Lifting a gloved hand, she waved and grinned.

Claire shook her head and returned her gaze to Ethan. "I hate to say it, but I have to go. I've made a mess of today. Between mounting the horse backward, stumbling through my speech, and turning the end of the match into an emergency room visit, I think the queen mother's ready to kill me. Oh, and then there's the microphone thing."

Ethan squeezed her hand and dipped his head closer

to hers. Lowering his voice, he whispered, "I think you did a wonderful job. I can't wait to see you tomorrow." Then, he released her hand.

Marching back to her seat, Claire heard the announcer overhead, "Please join me in a round of applause for Dr. Thomson. She not only entertainingly gave our welcoming remarks but took care of one of our riders."

The crowd burst into cheers as Claire arrived at the queen mother's side. Surprisingly, she said, "Well, done, my dear. You couldn't make me prouder."

With her grandmother's final remark, Claire considered the day a smashing success—microphone and all.

Chapter 9
March 22

Ethan stared at his reflection in the hall mirror and buttoned and unbuttoned his green short-sleeve shirt for the third time. He had stopped by his family's estate to drop off some paperwork before heading to the castle.

Ethan didn't know what to do with his hands, so he continued to fiddle with the top button of his shirt. His fingers trembled at the thought of seeing Claire again. Glancing at his watch, Ethan realized he needed to leave, or he'd be late for their date—at least he hoped she considered it a date. He sure did.

Exiting the house, Ethan slid into his black SUV as his father's silver luxury sedan pulled into the driveway.

His father glided out of his vehicle and made a circular gesture with his hand, indicating for Ethan to roll down the window.

Ethan gritted his teeth. He knew what his father wanted to say. At the polo match, Ethan had avoided a long conversation with Abigail and her family. Between the game itself and the excitement at the end with the injured player, Ethan only gave a brief hello to Abigail. He left amid the cheers for Claire at the game's conclusion and drove home ahead of his family. Then, he had headed to work.

Ethan acted as chief financial officer for his father's real estate business, so he hoped this excuse might suffice. The only thing his father cared about more than money was making more money. Still, his father viewed Abigail as more money, so perhaps he hadn't been pleased.

Judging by his father's frown at this moment, Ethan supposed the latter to be the case. *Great.* He rolled down the window and spoke in an even tone, "Father, what can I do for you? I'm in a hurry."

His father leaned down, resting his elbow on the car window's frame. With his hair slicked back and a steely look in his eyes, he looked like a man determined to get his way. "I'll tell you what you can do for me. You can explain that spectacle yesterday between you and the doctor and why you avoided Abigail and her family. Also, where are you in a rush to right now?"

Pulling his gaze away from his father's scrutiny, Ethan stared straight ahead. "I don't know what you're talking about between myself and Claire. Nothing happened. She's a lovely person from what I know about her and certainly beautiful and accomplished. I'm surprised it would upset you if something developed, given her potential position of power."

His father sneered. "Position of power—ha! That's rich. The Crown provides glamour, tradition, and charity, sure—but power?" He shook his head. "Parliament—that's where the power lies. The ability to make and change laws, to bend them to a more favorable outcome for ourselves and the family business. Don't forget that Abigail's family fortune stands at double that of the Crown's."

Ethan lifted his eyes to his father's. "So, that's it. Because Abigail has more money and power than Dr. Thomson, I'm to marry her. Abigail can't carry on a conversation, Father. She's boring and even spiteful at times."

"You still didn't answer my question. Where did you go last night, and where are you off to now?"

"Father, I'm a thirty-three-year-old man. I don't live at home any longer even though I spend a lot of time here for business—I have my apartment I rent, remember? Last night I did go to the real estate office to finish some work." Dodging his father's question about his plans for the day, Ethan said, "Now, I must go, or I'll be late." He started the car, and his father stepped back from the window.

His father's eyes narrowed, but he didn't press the matter.

Ethan took this opportunity to leave and gunned the gas. His car shot off, and he couldn't get away from the family estate fast enough. The greater distance he put between himself and his father's expectations the quicker his anger would recede. His heart rate did not slow, though, as his thoughts turned to Claire. Perhaps, she could help heal his heart and mend the wounds his father's constant disapproval inflicted.

~

Ethan's strapping figure approached from across the lawn. Dressed in khakis and a fitted green polo t-shirt unbuttoned at the top, which revealed his muscular, thick neck, he took long strides. His light hair glinted in the sunlight, and when he caught Claire's gaze, his blue eyes lit up, and he waved.

As he neared her, his smile softened. "Albert let me in and told me I could come back to the gardens on my own. He said you'd be out here. I hope it's okay."

She grinned. "It's okay. I'm glad to see you. I thought we could take a walk along the outer garden walkway. It's part of the garden I've never explored, and it looks like the weather will be perfect."

His smile widened, and he extended an arm to her.

How chivalrous. Claire wrapped her hands around his strong upper arm, and her face warmed. Somehow, even though they'd only spoken to one another a few times, she felt at ease with him—as if they'd known each other for years. He made her feel seen and beautiful.

They strolled along the pebbled path through a maze of boxwoods and aromatic flowers beginning to bloom. The bushes in some areas soared over six feet high, providing them with the rarity of privacy.

For several minutes neither of them spoke, though the quiet seemed comfortable. Finally, Claire broke the silence, "I enjoyed the polo match yesterday. Your riding looked incredible. I'm amazed anyone can ride a horse and do anything else. I had a hard time simply staying on top of mine."

His eyes widened. "What are you talking about? You were the incredible one yesterday. You fixed that rider's arm in two seconds and didn't even break a sweat. After you left, all the guys said how smart and gorgeous you were."

Claire could feel her face warming. She pressed a hand to her cheek. "Oh, stop. They did not."

He nodded. "They did, and they were right."

Claire didn't have to touch her cheek this time to

know it was red. "Well, thank you. I love medicine. It's been the hardest part about being here. I miss standing in the OR, performing surgery on a patient—surgery makes sense to me. If there's something broken, I can fix it. Here—" she gestured around herself, "in this royal world, I don't feel like I know anything, and I haven't fixed anything besides your friend's arm. I've probably broken several things—the microphone for one."

Ethan stared at her for a second and then chuckled. He continued walking. "You have to find the humor in it. At least it livened up an otherwise boring match."

"True." Claire grinned.

He glanced at her as if considering whether to say something. "Do you mind if I ask you a question?"

She hesitated before answering, "Sure."

"You have this amazing career, beauty, and a life elsewhere. What would make you want to give up everything in your old life to take the throne as queen of Amorley? To me, it seems like a suffocating position with too many rules and responsibilities. Plus, would you be able to continue practicing medicine?"

She lifted her eyes to his and stopped walking. "Wow, those are important questions. Questions I've asked myself every day since I found out about my father."

"Found out what about your father?" He raised a brow.

"Found out that my father never knew about my existence. He didn't know that my mother, whom I loved dearly and who passed away a little over a year ago, hid me from him for all these years. I know she tried to protect me, but I always believed my father didn't want me. Coming here gives me the opportunity to find out more about him and my family. Even though he's not here, getting to see pictures from his life and ask the queen mother questions helps—at least somewhat."

He took her hands in his. "I'm glad. I can understand your wanting to learn about your father. In many ways, I don't feel like I know my father at all, either. He definitely doesn't understand me."

"Your father's hard on you? Lots of expectations?"

He nodded, taking a step closer. "Lots. I work for his real estate company, and I enjoy my job, but he doesn't only want to be my boss at work. He wants to dictate my entire life."

Claire leaned in further to Ethan, with only inches separating their faces. "I'm sorry. That must be hard."

Ethan shrugged and dropped one of her hands. He pushed a loose tendril away from her face. "You have the most beautiful eyes."

A smile tugged at the corner of her lips, and she peered up at him through her lashes. "Thank you." Claire closed her eyes and tilted her head upward. She could feel his breath near her lips. A gunshot fired overhead, startling her. Claire jumped back, and her hand flew to her chest. "What was that?"

Another gunshot fired. Someone called, "Pull." A third shot fired.

"Clay pigeon shooting," Ethan answered, matter-of-factly.

A sigh escaped Claire's lips. "Oh, good. I thought someone might have tried to murder us for trespassing."

He laughed and shook his head. "No, it's only someone with a gun and a penchant for ruining a great moment."

Claire smiled, then noticed the time on her wristwatch. "I'm late for tea with my grandmother. I hate to cut our walk short, but I have to go. If I miss a Royal Lesson, she'll torture me with some awful task like naming every spoon in the silver tray."

"Well, I'd hate for anyone to spend the evening naming spoons, so we'd better head back." Grinning, Ethan took her hand in his again and led her up the path toward the castle. When they arrived at the rear entrance, he stopped and turned to face her. Leaning forward, he kissed her on the cheek. "Thank you for the walk. I can't wait to see you again."

Claire grinned. She couldn't wait, either. "Thank you. I overheard my grandmother talking about some Head of State Dinner I have to attend. Would you be available next Saturday night to attend as my escort? It's here at the castle in the Grand Banquet Room. I promise not to use any microphones this time."

He squeezed her hand and released it. "I'd be honored. See you then." Ethan gave her one last smile before walking up the stairs and down the Great Hall.

As she stared after him, Queen Maurelle's sharp voice interrupted Claire's thought, "My, my, it looks like things are heating up between the two of you. Isn't that Ethan, James Kane's son?"

Clare took a few cautious steps closer to Maurelle. "I don't know if I'd say heating up, but yes, that is Ethan. Why do you ask?"

Her stepmother's expression shifted. She looked gleeful. "Oh, no reason. Did your grandmother mention anything about his family to you?" She stared at her fingernails.

Claire transferred her weight to the other foot. "Uh, no. I don't think so."

Maurelle met her gaze. "Oh, good. Well, enjoy your afternoon." She turned to leave, but Milo bounded down the hallway and nearly knocked her over.

Albert trailed behind him with an empty leash in hand, waving his arms in the air and yelling, "Milo, Milo, come here. Stop. I demand you stop at once."

As if understanding Albert's wishes, Milo planted himself in a seated position at Claire's ankle. He glanced up at her, his tongue hanging out the side of his mouth.

Maurelle shrieked, "That mangy, filthy animal. He almost made me fall, and he's torn the edge of my dress." She pointed at a small hole at the bottom of her emerald gown.

Squinting at the imperceptible snag, Claire gulped. "I'm sorry he ran into you, but he's a dog. Dogs do that. He didn't mean to do it—he's full of energy."

Milo seemed to understand the queen's displeasure and turned his gaze toward her. His demeanor shifted, and he gave a low, rumbling growl. Milo had discernment; Claire had to give that much to him.

"Young lady, I'd advise you to keep a better handle on your mutt. Keep him out of my way. You wouldn't want him to get hurt, and this castle contains many dangerous things."

Claire shivered.

Her stepmother spun on her heel and sashayed away down the same hallway as Ethan. This time, watching the retreating figure caused a wave of nausea to surge through Claire's chest. She didn't know what Maurelle knew, but Claire had a feeling she'd soon find out, and she didn't look forward to it—not one bit.

Chapter 10
Ten days until The Royal Gala

Claire sat at the writing desk in her room, shifting through some photographs of her father that the queen mother had given her. One of the photographs showed him in a black suit, and her mother dressed up in a white sundress. They smiled and looked deeply in love. Maybe the picture came from their secret wedding. The queen mother had told her she found it in the back of one of her son's journals after he passed.

Tracing the two faces in the picture with her fingers, Claire didn't notice when her granny walked up behind her.

Placing a hand on her shoulder, Granny leaned her head closer to see what Claire had in her hand. "Ah, your mother was gorgeous. You look so much like her, but I see a lot of your father in you, too. You have his eyes—kind eyes."

Turning her head toward Granny, Claire smiled. "Thanks. What did I get from you?"

Her granny's eyes flashed, and she wore a mischievous smile. "Why, my sassy spunk—you simply haven't fully broken yours out yet, but you will. It's in there." She pointed to Claire's chest. "I know it."

Claire shook her head and chuckled. "I don't know,

Granny. I think you've got enough spunk for the two of us." She shuffled the photos into a neat stack and shoved them into the desk drawer along with the letter she'd received from Halford. The university's letterhead peeked out from the top.

Granny pointed toward the letter as Claire tucked it away. "What's that?"

Staring at her hands in her lap for a second, Claire let the words she'd avoided all day tumble out, "It's a letter from Halford University. They've officially offered me a position on staff as an orthopedic surgeon. I'd get to conduct research studies and work at the most elite medical institution in the United States."

"Then, why are you so sad? Isn't this what you've wanted for the past ten years or so?"

Claire lifted her eyes to meet her granny's. "It is...but this makes everything real. According to this letter, I have to decide in ten days if I'm accepting the job. I'd need to be there after finishing the remainder of my fellowship in a few months. By this summer, I could be living and working at my dream school."

Granny stepped back and narrowed her eyes. "I'm still not seeing the problem, unless it's because of a certain hunky man that's escorting you to this dinner in the next fifteen minutes. I overheard old Queenie Maurelle discussing Ethan after he left the other day. She said that anyone who takes the throne must marry someone of nobility. It sounded like a no-commoners-allowed type of thing. Of course, you're a half-commoner, so what does she know? Have you mentioned Ethan to the queen mother? What does she think of him?"

Subtlety didn't suit Granny. Claire frowned. "I

haven't talked about him with her yet. He does complicate things. I have a choice to make. I'm starting to care about Amorley and all," she emphasized all, "its people. Yes, I like Ethan a lot, but I've also worked so hard to achieve my career goals. I love surgery, and I still don't see how I'd be able to take the throne and run the country while carrying a full caseload of patients. I mentioned that bit to my grandmother, and she didn't seem thrilled at the idea of me working in an OR part-time as queen."

Granny shrugged. "Well, then tell them they can keep their tiara...or crown...or whatever they use here. You and I can hop a plane back home, and I'll get back to playing bingo before you can blink."

She'd have to say goodbye to Ethan. Claire's shoulders sagged.

Her grandmother narrowed her eyes. "Of course, the other option is to become the queen of Amorley and tell them you're going to continue doing surgery and seeing patients part-time. Since you'll be queen, they'll have to say it's okay. Then, you get that young man to propose to you and—bam," she clapped her hands, "happily ever after. Well, almost. I don't know what you're going to do with that stepmother of yours. At least she behaves herself when Milo comes around. She knows he's not a fan of hers."

Claire giggled. "Granny, that's not nice—but you're right. Milo tends to demonstrate an excellent judge of character." She glanced at the small crystal and gold clock on the desk. "We need to head downstairs. The dinner will start soon, and if I'm not there for the Entry, or whatever grandmother called it, then I might fail Royal Lessons."

Her grandmother snorted. "We wouldn't want that."

Sending her granny a grin, Claire rose from her seat and offered the older woman her arm. "I still want to do a good job while I'm here. I don't know what I'm going to do with my future, but this country, this castle, and this family meant a lot to my father. I need to make him proud."

Margaret Thomson patted her granddaughter's hand as they exited the room to begin their descent downstairs to the Great Hall. "He'd be proud of you, kiddo."

~

Claire walked towards Ethan down the Great Hall. When his eyes fell upon her, he caught his breath. She appeared stunning wearing a sky blue strapless ballgown, looking every bit the future queen of Amorley. Claire wore her hair up, revealing her long neck and creamy skin.

As Claire approached him, his breath quickened, and he tried to calm his nerves. "You are gorgeous. Simply beautiful. It's an honor to escort you tonight."

She smiled and waved away his compliment. "Oh, I feel silly. I never wear high heels at home, and I'm afraid I'll trip and fall."

He smiled, offering her his arm. "That's why you have me here to steady you." Staring into her eyes, he promised, "I won't let you fall."

She accepted his arm and gave a slight nod. "Okay."

The pair approached the entrance to the Grand Banquet Room.

The queen mother stood waiting for Claire. Her gaze settled on Ethan, and a smile that started to form on her lips settled into a thin line.

Ethan leaned his head closer to Claire's and whispered, "Did your grandmother know that I would be your escort tonight? She doesn't look happy."

Claire glanced at her and then returned her attention to Ethan. She squeezed his arm. "I'm sure it's okay. I didn't get a chance to tell her earlier about you because of all the preparations around the castle for the evening, but she told me I could invite someone. I guess Granny counts as someone, but she's been here all along. She's growing on the queen mother, too. Granny adds a lot of color to any event she attends."

Ethan peered ahead and saw Claire's granny chatting up Albert as she waited in line. She ribbed Albert and chuckled, tossing her head back and causing her big light blue hat to fall to the ground.

Albert picked it up and returned it to Granny, completing her matching monochromatic ensemble of blue pants and a blue sequin top.

Ethan grinned. "I like Granny. She's got spunk."

Claire smiled at him. "I think she likes you, too."

Albert stepped forward and entered the Grand Banquet Room to announce the royal family and their escorts. Albert had volunteered to escort Granny, likely so she wouldn't make a spectacle on her own. The invited members from Parliament, as well as other heads of state, sat awaiting them. An additional twenty or thirty chairs flanked the long dining table tonight.

Albert read from a list each royal's name, and when he got to Ethan and Claire, he paused.

Ethan thought he saw Albert wink at them. He relaxed his shoulders a bit.

"Presenting Dr. Claire Isabel Thomson and her

escort, the Earl of Abbingdon, Ethan Kane."

Ethan kept his eyes forward, his chin lifted, and he took a step.

Claire didn't budge.

He glanced at her.

Her eyes widened, and her mouth dropped open slightly. She clamped it shut, and Ethan saw a questioning look in her eyes.

Ethan knew he should have mentioned his title sooner. He didn't get to tell Claire about his family during their walk in the garden. The roomful of guests waited for the pair to take their seats so the dinner could begin. Ethan tilted his head. "We should sit down," he whispered.

Albert reread their names, now wearing a quizzical look, "Ahem, Dr. Claire Isabel Thomson and her escort, the Earl of Abbingdon, Ethan Kane."

Claire gave a nod and took a step forward.

Ethan guided her to the two open seats near the queen mother and across from Queen Maurelle. Pulling her chair out for her, he bent down and whispered in her ear, "I'll explain later. I'm sorry."

She still looked shocked but sent him a smile. Claire lifted her napkin from the salad plate and unfolded it from the complicated configuration of a swan. Placing the linen in her lap, she murmured, "Okay."

~

Claire couldn't believe it—*Ethan held a title. Earl of Abbingdon.* That meant one less obstacle for their future together. When she'd heard his name and title read aloud, she'd felt shocked and a little hurt that he hadn't told her but mostly relieved. After her conversation with Granny upstairs about Ethan, her job, and the choices she had to make, Claire's stomach had twisted in knots.

Then, Claire saw the queen mother's face when she and Ethan entered the Grand Banquet Room. Did her grandmother's expression result from Ethan's non-royal status? None of that mattered to Claire, but Granny had said it mattered to the royal family, and maybe Granny had a point. *Why did the queen mother seem displeased with Ethan?*

The queen mother rose from her seat, and all chatter hushed. "Thank you for joining my family to celebrate this wonderful country and its leaders with the Head of State Dinner. Please enjoy the meal and thank you to those who serve our country and its people well." She lowered herself into her seat, and the quiet chatter and clinking of glasses resumed.

Waitstaff bustled around the table, filling water goblets, delivering salads, and keeping the tables clean.

Queen Maurelle sat across from Claire. She lifted a fork to her ruby red lips, then paused. Her eyes flitted to Ethan, and her mouth formed a grin as if she had a secret. Returning the fork to its place next to her plate, Maurelle addressed Claire's date, "Ethan, or should I say, Earl, it's kind of you to join us this evening."

Ethan sent Maurelle an uncertain smile. "Thank you. It's an honor to escort Dr. Thomson." He looked at Claire, and his smile warmed.

Claire felt pleased by his attention and anxious about where the conversation with her stepmother might lead. She didn't trust the woman—not at all.

Her stepmother continued, "I must say, it surprised me to see you here with Claire. I would have thought your father, the duke, would disapprove." She folded her hands together and leaned closer. "Don't worry. I won't tell him you came tonight as the future queen's date instead of attending with Lady Abigail Fulton. Everyone knows about that arrangement. It's peculiar, though, why your father might want you to marry her instead of the future queen of Amorley." She tapped one of her red talons to her chin. "Hmm... it's perplexing, for sure."

Maurelle didn't seem perplexed at all. Claire's stepmother looked like she'd dropped that breadcrumb on purpose. It did make Claire's thoughts whirl. *Did Ethan have a girlfriend? Why did his father not attend the Head of State Dinner if he held the title of duke?* Many of the country's nobility and Parliament had come tonight. *Why hadn't he?* She'd have to pose these questions to Ethan later.

Once again, Milo saved the day. He dashed through the Grand Banquet Room's entrance, and this time he brought a present. Inside his mouth, he carried a dead bird—at least Claire prayed it was dead.

He rounded the entire table at full speed twice, escaping the maneuvers of several waiters and Albert.

Claire started to jump from her seat and corral him but glanced at the queen mother first.

Her grandmother gave a firm shake of her head.

Claire called for Milo twice, but he'd worked himself into a frenzy and seemed to enjoy his dinner debut too much to listen. Finally, when Claire considered slinking under the table in a puddle of embarrassment, Milo stopped next to Maurelle's chair.

Milo spat out the carcass on the bottom of her stepmother's dress and lifted his head, smiling. He panted, his tongue dripping saliva, looking pleased with himself and his performance.

Bolting from her seat, Maurelle screamed, "Get him out of here! Right now. That mutt has it in for me. I know he does. I cannot believe we allowed her to bring him here. Look what he's done. He's dropped a…a dead bird on my dress. It's ruined."

Her shrieks caused an absolute silence to settle throughout the room.

Claire suspected the other diners and waitstaff feared saying the first word. Closing her eyes, Claire drew in a breath and released it slowly before speaking, "Queen Maurelle, I apologize for Milo. He didn't mean to upset you, I'm sure." She was not sure. Animals did have a funny way of knowing about the goodness of people.

Recognizing Claire's voice, Milo trotted around the table and lay down next to her, exhausted from his fun.

Maurelle hissed, "I want him out of here. Ten days is too long. I demand you remove him from the castle this instant."

Rising from her seat, the queen mother placed her clasped hands in front of her chest. "Now, Maurelle, I do think you're overreacting a bit." She glanced at her granddaughter. "I can't say a dog's place is at the Head of State Dinner. However, I agreed to let my granddaughter keep Milo here, so he is our guest, too." She peered at Maurelle again. "I might remind you that my hope and belief is Claire will be with us well past ten days. I believe she will guide this country for many years to come." Then, the queen mother took her seat and nodded at Albert. "Albert, please take Sir Milo to the kitchen and find him something more appropriate to eat. Oh, and remove the bird if you will. Thank you."

Albert didn't look excited about the prospect of retrieving the bird, but he obliged, picking it up by the tail and then grabbing Milo's collar to guide him out of the room.

Claire flashed Albert a smile before he left, grateful for his help.

He shook his head.

Super. The night had started with a bang, and Claire feared she would never make a good queen, much less in as little as ten days.

Ethan leaned his head next to hers.

She felt his warm breath by her ear, and it sent a tingle down her spine.

"Ten days?" he asked.

Claire's chest tightened, and her throat ached. "Sort of…yes. Ten days, but we can talk about that later, too." It looked like she'd have a lot to discuss with him after dinner.

Queen Maurelle sat down again but stared at Claire throughout the dinner with loathing in her eyes.

Claire gulped. Ten days—not enough time with the man who'd captured her heart and too long to navigate the entanglements of living under the same roof as her stepmother. *Perhaps, fairytales were right. There was an evil queen in every story.* Claire wondered when the dragon would arrive and if Ethan could slay it for her.

~

Claire walked down the stairs from the castle's rear entrance leading to the garden.

Ethan intertwined his fingers in Claire's and led her down the pebbled path.

The stars overhead cast a golden canopy above the garden below, and the crisp early spring air nipped at

Claire's bare arms. She shivered and rubbed them.

Glancing down at Claire, Ethan frowned. "You're cold. I'm sorry. Here, take my dinner jacket." He dropped her hand and shrugged out of his coat, placing it around her shoulders. He pulled the coat closed and rubbed her arms. Leaving his hands on her shoulders, he stared into her eyes. "I feel like I should explain about my family and my title."

She gazed up at him, and her shivering subsided. "Okay, but only if you'll let me explain about the ten days."

He grinned. "Sure." He dropped his head, looking to the ground before returning his gaze to Claire's. "It's true. I'm an earl and the future duke of Abbingdon. My family owns many real estate holdings and land, and my father's family did have an immense fortune at one time. Over the years, my father made a few bad investments and had to sell some of the properties. Much of the fortune vanished. Don't mistake me; I will inherit a sizable sum, and it's more than enough for me. Money holds no importance to me, but to my father, money trumps everything—me, his family, even love."

Claire saw sadness in Ethan's eyes, and she lifted a hand to his cheek. "That can't be true. How could anyone choose money over love?"

Ethan lifted his hand to hers. "It's true. That's fine for him, but not for me. I want to marry for love—I want a family, an honest living, and that's all. My father wants me to marry Lady Abigail Fulton. Her family's wealth surpasses everyone's in Amorley, including the royal family's. That's why the queen said those things about Abigail. My father expects me to marry her and give him an advantage both financially and politically. Her father holds the highest seat in Parliament and can make land dealings more advantageous for my father."

Claire dropped her hand from his cheek and looked away. "I see."

He took her hands in his again and reassured her, "I'm not going to let that happen. I refuse to marry her, and my father knows it, but he thinks he can threaten me about stripping away my title or inheritance and force me to do what he wants. Richard would love that. He's been eyeing the firstborn role since he came out of the womb."

Claire gave a wry laugh. "I can see that." She furrowed her brow. "What did the queen mean about your father not coming to the castle? What do you think that was about?"

He shrugged. "Who knows? My father does little that makes sense to me. I can't imagine why he wouldn't want to attend tonight and soak in the pomp and ceremony, but I quit trying to figure him out long ago."

Claire stepped closer and lifted her eyes to Ethan again. "I have a decision to make. In ten days, the queen mother wants to present me at the Royal Gala to the country as the official heir to the Crown and begin the coronation proceedings. At that time, she will submit paperwork to Parliament for approval, and in a few months, crown me queen—if she thinks I'm ready and if I accept. However, I'd likely have to give up my medical practice. Queen Maurelle mentioned something about marrying a noble, and I didn't know about your title—not that it matters to me. It doesn't, but I didn't know if the queen mother would allow us to date or if

I'd have to decide that as well. I've had a lot to think about."

"I know you'd make a great queen. You're kind, smart, and beautiful. Amorley would be fortunate to have you on the throne."

She shook her head. "I don't know if I can do it, Ethan. All of this royal stuff overwhelms me. I feel like just when I get the hang of it, disaster strikes. Take tonight—my dog brought roadkill to a state dinner—not good."

He laughed. "No, not good—you're right, but not a disaster. It takes time to learn something new, and you're discovering the expectations for your role as queen as well as learning about a family you didn't know existed. Give yourself some grace." He stepped closer.

She smiled up at him, and her heart pounded. "Thanks. I'll try."

"If you want, I can speak with a friend of mine in Parliament. I'm sure there's a loophole or some way you can continue to practice medicine while taking the throne. Even if you did medical work part-time, at least you wouldn't have to abandon something you love."

A few inches separated their lips. "Right," Claire breathed. "I wouldn't want to abandon something I love."

Ethan placed his hand on her cheek and caressed it.

She closed her eyes and tilted her chin upward.

He grazed his lips against hers, hesitant at first, but then his kiss deepened in intensity.

Claire melted into his embrace and allowed the walls she'd built around her heart to crumble. She'd never expected to find love, much less in Amorley, but

Ethan surprised her. He exceeded all expectations. Claire prayed that if she entrusted him with her heart, he wouldn't break it.

Chapter 11
One Week until the Royal Gala

Ethan sat behind the desk in his office at Kane Real Estate and Land Holdings, Inc. and answered the phone. "Hello, this is Ethan Kane."

Ethan's old university mate, Michael, spoke with enthusiasm, "Ethan, I got your message. How are you doing? It's been a long time."

"Too long. We should plan to meet up again soon. Have dinner or something."

"Absolutely. What can I do for you?"

Ethan stared out the window in his office and saw the sun peeking through the clouds. The sunlight warmed his face and made him hopeful. "I'm sorry to bother you, but I hoped you might look into something for me."

"Sure, happy to help. What is it?" Michael asked.

"I've gotten to know Dr. Claire Thomson. She's next in line for the Crown, as I'm sure you've heard, and she hopes to practice medicine at least part-time if she accepts the position. With you working in Parliament and having your law degree, I hoped you might look into the matter and see if the constitution permits her to do both."

"I see. I don't think a precedent exists for this

situation, but I'll look into it. However, the coronation oath does state that the person accepting the honor and privilege of the Crown must relinquish all other endeavors and concerns and dedicate themselves to the country of Amorley."

Ethan tapped his finger on the desk. "I know. The queen mother has expressed her concern that Claire couldn't rule the country and pursue her medical interests. She thinks Claire has to choose. I'm hoping you can find a loophole so the queen mother can take it to Parliament and get it approved. It would help make Claire's choice for her."

Michael cleared his throat. "It sounds like Dr. Thomson means a lot to you. I thought I heard from your father that you and Abigail Fulton were an item."

His neck burning, Ethan tucked his phone between his ear and shoulder and shuffled some papers on his desk. "You heard wrong. My father might say otherwise, but I'm not attached to anyone officially."

His friend chuckled. "Are you sure about that?"

No. He'd become very attached to Claire but knowing it in his heart and admitting it out loud remained two different matters. *What if she returned to Boston? What if she picked her old life over him and all the pressures and constraints of royal life? What if she became the queen of Amorley and they still couldn't be together?* "I don't know," Ethan replied.

"It sounds like you do, especially if you're going to all this trouble for her."

Ethan glanced toward the window again, wishing all the problems with his family and the obstacles between him and Claire would vanish. "Thanks for checking on this for me. As soon as you find out anything, give me a call. I appreciate it."

"No problem. Glad we had a chance to talk. Let's take the horses out sometime soon."

Ethan returned his gaze to the papers in front of him. His eyes focused on the title at the top: Coronation Oath of Amorley. "That sounds great. Thanks again, Michael. Goodbye." He hung up the call and placed his phone on the desk. Staring at the bold black words made the future seem more daunting and uncertain. The date for the Royal Gala loomed—seven days away. That didn't leave much time—not much time at all.

~

Claire read the letter from Halford University for the umpteenth time:

Halford University School of Medicine and Research
253 Oakmont Drive 01451

Dr. Claire Thomson
243 New England Way
Boston, Massachusetts 01451

Dr. Thomson,
    Thank you for your interest in Halford University. I am happy to extend a position in the Orthopedic Surgery Program as a Surgeon, Adjunct Professor and Researcher to you. Please inform us of your acceptance no later than April 11. We look forward to the possibility of working with you in the future.
Sincerely,
Ulrich Mendelton, Chief of Orthopedic Surgery

Halford University

Claire had thought about the words "Adjunct Professor" several times since reading the letter. Adjunct Professor meant giving lectures, and that meant public speaking. She'd hoped to avoid that sort of thing. Claire couldn't escape it—if she took the throne, there'd be loads of public speaking—charity events, special galas, political dinners—and if she took the post in Boston, she'd have a regular date with a podium and a lecture hall. Claire sighed and folded the letter into thirds and stuffed it in her blue wool coat pocket.

The wind blew hard, and she pulled her coat tighter around her. Gazing out toward the horizon, Claire closed her eyes, bowed her head, and said a prayer for God to tell her what to do. Who was she? For years Claire thought of herself as a fatherless daughter. Finding out the truth about her father and her parents' past meant one thing—she had to figure out who she was now and what she needed in her life. Was she a queen? A doctor? Both? Would she have to choose love or country?

Footsteps clicked against the pebbled pathway behind Claire, and she turned to see who approached.

"Claire, what are you doing standing out here in the cold?" Her stepmother took a few strides closer.

Claire crossed her arms in front of her chest. "I needed some fresh air."

Maurelle narrowed her eyes as if she suspected more to the reason for Claire's solitary ponderance. "I see. Well, I'm glad I found you. I thought you should know that your dog—Milo, is it?"

Claire tilted her head. "Yes, Milo. What about

him?"

Maurelle moved nearer. "It seems he ran off around lunchtime. I believe Albert said he let the dog outside to relieve himself." She furrowed her brow and spat out the word *relieve*. "It appears he never returned. Albert and a few members of the house staff searched the grounds for him, but they have not found him anywhere."

Claire's chest tightened. Milo and Granny had been her only family for the past year. She wouldn't have survived the loss of her mother without Milo. Claire didn't view him as a pet—he remained to this day her best friend. She shot her eyes to the queen's. "I've got to go find him. Where could he have gone?"

Tilting her head toward a thick forest at the edge of the Royal Gardens, Maurelle continued, "That's why I'm here. I realize we haven't gotten off to the best start. I hope to change that. Why don't you and I take a ride to the forest and see if we can find him? There's so much ground to cover that I think horseback would be the best option." She arched one brow. "What do you say?"

Claire stared at the queen's face and paused, considering her choices. She could go inside to the castle's warmth and hope Milo would find his way home, or she could venture into the forest with a possible adversary. Claire still didn't know if she trusted Maurelle, but she had to find her dog. After a few seconds, Claire nodded. "Okay. Let's go."

The two women hurried to the stables, and an attendant helped them saddle and bridle the horses.

Claire tried to recall how to mount her horse, a brown thoroughbred who kept casting hesitant glances at her. She patted his side. "Don't worry. I'm nice. I'm not going to hurt you. You can trust me." Placing her hands on the saddle, Claire counted in her head to three, and swung her leg over as she'd done at the polo match. This time she landed the correct way. Claire smiled. At least she'd improved at some of this royal stuff.

Maurelle stood ahead of her and mounted her horse more gracefully and in only a few seconds. Petting his neck, she cooed, "That's a good boy." She glanced over her shoulder to Claire and asked, "Aren't horses lovely? Much smarter than other animals and less allergy-inducing for me." Looking at Claire, Maurelle raised her forehead. "Ready?"

Nodding, Claire pulled in a deep breath, then released it. "Ready."

The pair rode in silence for five to ten minutes, but once they reached the edge of the Royal Gardens, Maurelle called, "Follow me."

Claire obliged and let her horse trail behind Maurelle's into the darkened forest. The days had grown longer, but twilight still began early in the evening. What had looked like late afternoon sun quickly turned to dim shadows in the thick woods. Large oak trees provided a canopy, and with the sun setting, Claire shivered. She wished she'd brought a hat and gloves...and a flashlight.

"Do you know where we're going? We won't get lost, will we?" Claire asked.

Maurelle shook her head. "Stay close, though. These woods run deep, and if you get separated from me, I doubt you'd find your way back easily."

This statement could have sounded like a threat, but Claire chastised herself for thinking the worst about her stepmother, who had offered to help. Claire yelled, "Milo. Milo. Are you here, boy? Milo, come. Milo, please come." Her eyes scanned the bushes and undergrowth, praying she'd see his blond fur and wagging tail trying to dig out a rabbit or mole. Trying again, Claire screamed so loud her voice cracked, "Milo? Milo, come." Panic rose in her chest, and tears stung her eyes. What if she didn't find him? *What if he never returned*? She couldn't lose him, too.

While Claire shouted and searched, she'd lost sight of Maurelle. Assuming her stepmother had gone ahead, Claire thought she would catch up to her. After circling her horse and looking around the forest, Claire found herself alone. "Maurelle?" she called for her stepmother in a soft voice. When she received no answer, her hands began to shake. She cupped her hands around her mouth. "Maurelle? Where are you? I don't see you."

The wind whistling through the trees provided the only response.

Racking sobs took hold, and Claire laid her head in her hands, still holding the reins, and cried. She wept harder than she had in months, shedding tears for all of the past year's losses.

Claire shouldn't have left Milo alone in the castle. She shouldn't have let Maurelle talk her into coming to the forest. She shouldn't have come here at all and tried to become a princess. So many things she shouldn't have done.

When she had almost given up all hope of finding Milo, she heard rustling in the woods. Quieting her tears, she listened. The rustling grew louder. It sounded like hoofbeats accompanied the rustling now, too. "Hello? Is anybody there? Maurelle?"

Claire wiped the tears from her cheeks with the back of one hand and tried to clear her eyes. Gazing ahead, she saw a man on horseback, and with him a—

"Woof," sounded a bark.

Claire felt her face break into a wide grin. She shouted, "Milo, you're okay." She hopped off her horse and landed on her feet before dashing toward her furry friend.

He bounded into her arms and knocked her on her back.

Laughing happily, Claire welcomed his wet kisses. "Milo, I thought I'd never see you again." She opened her eyes to Ethan's face standing over her. "What are you doing here?"

He extended a hand to her. "I must have arrived at the castle around the time you headed off with Queen Maurelle. When I asked Albert where to find you, he said Milo had gone missing, and you and your stepmother went looking for him."

She accepted his hand and rose, dusting debris off her clothes. "I cannot believe you found me...and Milo."

He picked a few rogue sticks and leaves from Claire's hair, his hand lingering at the base of her neck. "Another waitstaff told me you'd headed toward the stables, and a stable hand informed me about your trek to the woods. With it getting dark, I became worried and thought you might need help. These woods are dangerous at night—lots of wild animals and the temperature drops. I hunted around for maybe ten or fifteen minutes, and Milo came running through the trees, barking and happy to see me."

She smiled at him and gave him a fierce hug.

Laying her head against his chest, Claire whispered, "Thank you. Thank you so much." Tears filled her eyes and spilled over. "I don't know what I would have done if I'd lost Milo for good. He and Granny are all I have left, and he's been the man in my life for…well, forever."

Ethan leaned back and gently raised her chin with his fingertips. He brushed away her tears with his thumb and shook his head, his mouth settling into a serious line. "That's not true—the part about him and Granny being all you have…you have God…and you have me. You have all of me—all of my heart." Before more tears had a chance to fall, Ethan cupped her face in his hands and pressed his lips firmly against hers.

All of Claire's fears melted, and for the first time in a year, she had hope. She let Ethan kiss away the doubt she'd carried for years about her worth. He'd offered her his heart—and she'd be foolish not to take it.

After several heart-pounding minutes, Ethan pulled away and planted a final soft kiss on Claire's cheek.

She raised one hand to her cheek and placed the other on his chest. "You have mine, too," she whispered. Now she needed to find a way to get everything she wanted—medicine, Amorley, and Ethan. Still filled with more questions than answers, Claire bent down and scooped Milo into a hug. She scratched his head and prayed for God to provide solutions.

Ethan collected Claire's horse and brought it to her. He handed her the reins. "We'd better go. They may send a search party out for you if we don't return soon. I'm sure your stepmother made it back to the castle by now and let them know you went missing."

Claire frowned. "You're right. I don't want to worry anyone." Before mounting her horse for what she hoped was the last time for a long while, she turned to Ethan and took a step closer. Placing one last kiss on his cheek, she murmured in his ear, "Thank you, again— for everything."

He nodded and grinned. "You're welcome." Then, he helped her onto her horse and mounted his own.

Claire followed behind him, weaving through the dark forest, but a nagging concern tugged at her thoughts. If Ethan had found her with ease, why hadn't Queen Maurelle? Had her stepmother left her on purpose? Was Maurelle responsible for Milo's disappearance? These questions turned over in her mind as she rode to the castle, but once the outline of Evercliff appeared, the troubling questions faded away. Her relief over finding Milo and hearing Ethan's affirming words replaced them. Things would work out—they had to.

~

Ethan arrived at Evercliff Castle's stables, hopped off the horse he'd borrowed, and handed the reins to the stable hand. He thanked him and patted the steed on the neck, offering his appreciation to the animal, too.

Turning, he walked up to Claire's horse and reached both hands to her waist. Encircling it, he eased her down to the ground and couldn't ignore their proximity. His pulse quickened, and it surprised him how easily she'd captured his heart. He wanted to stand with her longer but reasoned that everyone in the castle still thought Claire and Milo were missing, so instead, he suggested, "Why don't we head inside and let them know everyone is safe. Maybe we could grab a cup of tea...or coffee for you."

She sent him a teasing grin. "That sounds good. You still haven't won me over to the tea side."

He chuckled. "Oh, I know. I'm not giving up, though."

Claire called for Milo, "Come, Milo, follow me." She waved for the dog to join her as she headed to the castle's rear entrance.

Wearing a smile, Milo loped along behind his owner, looking happy to be home and not at all guilty for running away.

Claire, Ethan, and Milo hiked up a grassy knoll, now filling with dots of purple wildflowers.

Ethan opened the wooden door that provided entrance to the formal Royal Gardens and let Claire and Milo pass through first. He trailed behind them. "I almost forgot to tell you."

Claire whirled around to face him. "Tell me what?" She raised a brow.

"That I spoke with my old mate from school. He works in Parliament now and has a law degree. I thought he might have some ideas about how to get Parliament to approve your medical endeavors while also letting you accept the Crown."

Her eyes widened. "Does he think it's possible?"

He smiled and raised a hand. "I don't want to get ahead of ourselves, but Michael graduated first in his class, and if anyone can find a loophole, he can. He promised me he'd do his best and let me know something soon."

Claire sent him a smile. "Thank you for asking for me. I hope he finds a solution. I'd love to stay, but I couldn't bear giving up medicine. Without it, I don't know who I am or what I'd be—besides queen—and I'm not sure I'd be too good at that."

Ethan joined her and offered her his hand.

Claire placed her hand in his and stared at their interlocked fingers.

He squeezed her hand. "Hey, look at me."

Lifting her head, she found his gaze.

"I know you'd make an excellent queen. You can do it, and you have a whole team of people willing to help. I want you to have everything—medicine, the Crown, family, even me if you'll have me." He raised his forehead.

Claire nodded and bit her bottom lip. "Yes, of course. I want it all."

Squeezing her hand once more, he continued, "Good. Then, you shall get it."

They walked the rest of the way to Evercliff in silence. When they reached their destination, Albert stood at the top of the castle stairs near the back entrance.

Albert's eyes widened. "Ma'am. Ethan." He nodded at each of them. "Sir Milo is back, I see. Granny had a fit when she learned he'd gone missing. She insisted I send a search party out looking for him, which is what I was about to do." He turned his attention to the dog, who jumped up, planting his dirty paws on Albert's chest once again. "Sir Milo, where have you been?"

Milo licked his new friend's face, oblivious to the trouble he'd caused.

Claire clapped her hands. "Milo, sit."

The dog obliged and sank to the ground, lifting one leg to address an itch behind his ear, ignorant to his offense.

Peering at Albert, Claire sent him an apologetic smile. "Sorry about that, Albert." Her brow furrowed. "Is my stepmother back?"

Albert looked perplexed. "Ma'am, she arrived at the castle an hour ago. I believe she said she felt famished and told one of the waitstaff to bring her some tea and scones to the Grand Banquet Room. I haven't seen her since. I would imagine she's still there. Why do you ask?"

Claire's jaw dropped. She closed it and shook her head. "She went looking for Milo with me, and we lost track of one another. It's surprising she didn't tell you or someone that we'd become separated in the Dark Forest. I'm sure it's just a misunderstanding."

Albert looked uncertain. "I'm sure that's all it was…but ma'am, be careful. Another staff member mentioned that Queen Maurelle was the last person seen with Milo before he went missing. Still, I can't imagine she'd have arranged all this."

Ethan could imagine it—easily.

Claire turned to Ethan and placed a hand on his forearm. "Why don't I go speak with my stepmother, and you take Milo to Granny."

"Of course. I'll let Granny know you're both fine and have her tell the queen mother as well. If it's okay with you, I'll head out afterward so you can get some rest. I'd love to stay and spend more time with you, but you've had a long day."

Claire sent him a grin and thanked him.

He placed a quick kiss on her cheek and called to Milo, "Come on, Mr. Troublemaker. Let's get you some rest, too."

Milo trotted over to Ethan, looking like he'd had the

best day of his life.

Ethan shook his head but secretly thought this day might rank as one of the best in his life, too. Today, he'd given his heart to the woman he intended to marry. Now, Ethan needed to find a way to ensure she stayed in Amorley and didn't break his heart into a million pieces—and he had to keep a close watch on Maurelle. Ethan didn't trust her intentions, and he suspected if not for his arrival in the woods, Claire might have spent a cold, scary night alone in the Dark Forest.

~

Claire entered the Grand Banquet Room and found Queen Maurelle sitting at the far end of the table.

She'd taken time to change her clothes and wore a long, green gown with her hair pulled back in a tight bun. Seeing Claire in the doorway, Maurelle dabbed her napkin to her ruby lips and placed it on the table. "My dear, there you are."

There you are? Claire wanted to scream. *How could someone abandon another person in a deep, unfamiliar forest near nightfall*? She didn't know Maurelle's intentions, but she suspected her involvement in Milo's disappearance. Claire stared at the queen. "What happened to you?"

The queen rose from her seat and strode over, closing the space between her and Claire. "I got separated from you in the forest, and I called and called for you. After a while, I assumed you'd found Milo and made your way back to the castle on your own. Once I arrived here, I felt famished after all that activity, and one of the waitstaff told me Ethan had come to visit. I thought you'd gone off with him for a stroll, so I decided to eat something." She eyed Claire up and down, taking in her dirty, twig-filled appearance. "My, my, it looks like you had a rough time. It's a good thing you didn't get stranded in the Dark Forest overnight. It can be a dangerous place…lost in the woods."

Claire gritted her teeth, forcing herself to recall her Sunday school lessons as well as the manners her mother had taught her. "Yes, I can imagine the dangers of staying in the forest overnight. Thankfully, Ethan found Milo and me, so we're safe. Ethan saved the day in more ways than one."

Her stepmother narrowed her eyes. "Oh, really, how so?"

Claire took a step forward and jutted her chin out, challenging her stepmother. "He thinks he's found a way I can become the queen of Amorley and retain my medical practice. He also told me how much he cares for me. If I stay in Amorley, we can be together—a happily ever after."

Maurelle pursed her lips, and her eyes darkened. "Hmm. We shall see. I wouldn't get your hopes too high, my dear. Happily ever afters only exist in fairy tales. I'll tell you a secret about Ethan. His father, James, was your father's close childhood friend, and let's just say I don't think Ethan's father wants a linkage with the Crown."

"That's ridiculous. Who wouldn't want to see their son marry royalty? Not that it's important to me—it's not, but I cannot imagine why someone would have a problem with it."

The queen shrugged. "Maybe you're right, but now that I'm thinking on the matter—" she tapped her finger on her chin and continued, "isn't that the reason your mother left your father and cut off all ties between him and you? Isn't that why you didn't get to know your father—because of his future as the Crown?"

Claire's mouth went dry, and her shoulders sagged. Maurelle made a point. She hated to admit it, but that deep-seated fear circled Claire's thoughts as she lay in bed each night. If her mother didn't want anything to do with royalty, why would Ethan? Yes, he held a title, but did he want to subject himself to the scrutiny of the Crown?

"It's something to consider, my dear. Also, running a country isn't as easy as it looks. Wouldn't you rather become medical royalty at Halford instead of giving speeches and hosting dinners here? I don't want to dispel your ambitions, but we both know how the polo match opening remarks and the Head of State Dinner went. Then there's your dog."

Snapping her head up, Claire frowned. "What's wrong with my dog? Lots of kings and queens keep family pets. I've seen them in the tabloids."

Maurelle shook her head. "Not like yours. Milo appears too high-spirited for castle life. I'm afraid it won't work. You must admit if he stays here much longer, he's likely to get hurt."

Claire took a step toward her stepmother and narrowed her eyes. "Is that a threat?"

Smiling, Maurelle waved off the accusation. "No, my dear, I'm simply saying that perhaps the best place for you, Granny, and Milo might be at Halford University with your patients and your books. There's no shame in admitting that this endeavor was a mistake. Trust me, your father wouldn't have wanted to see you unhappy, and I'm sure your mother wouldn't have wanted to saddle you with the burden of royalty." She placed a hand on Claire's arm.

Shrinking away from the queen's touch, Claire straightened her posture. "You don't know what my mother would have wanted." She noticed a twig hanging from her hair out of the corner of her eye and paused her speech to remove it. "I know I'm not what the queen mother had in mind for a successor, but until I make my decision about taking the Crown, that's what I am—the successor. Thank you for your concern for me and my dog. Now, I'm going to take a hot shower and try to remove the Dark Forest remnants from my hair. Good evening." She spun on her heel and stormed out of the room, feeling proud that she'd stood up for herself. Claire still didn't know what she'd do about her future, but one thing she knew for sure–the queen would not bully her into leaving.

Chapter 12
Four days until the Royal Gala

Ethan had stayed at his apartment the past few days to avoid a confrontation with his father and to finish some work. He'd spoken to Claire, and they'd taken one brief stroll together since their adventure into the forest. Still, he hadn't seen her since then because the queen mother had kept her busy with Royal Lessons and preparations for the gala.

Today Ethan decided to brave breakfast with his family, and he prayed he'd find his father in a good mood. Their last interchange felt uncomfortable. He pulled up to the Kane Estate and turned off his car. Walking up the stairs to the stately manor, Ethan said one last prayer, straightened his tie, and smoothed his hair. He strode down the hallway to the parlor where his family usually ate breakfast. As soon as Ethan entered the room, tension filled the air. He stiffened.

James Kane sat at the head of the table with his hair slicked back, wire-rimmed glasses at the tip of his nose, and a ruddy complexion. When he saw Ethan walk into the room, he leaned back in his chair and crossed his arms in front of his chest. "Well, what do you have to say for yourself?"

Ethan took a few steps forward but didn't sit down. He glanced at his mother, but she averted her eyes, pretending to stare out the window. Thankfully, Richard hadn't joined his parents for breakfast, so Ethan didn't have to endure his brother's contribution to the impending argument. "What do you mean?"

His father's eyebrows furrowed. He yanked his glasses off his face, flung them on the table, and picked up a newspaper, shaking it in the air. "This! What do you have to say for yourself about this?"

Ethan circled the table, stopping next to his father's seat, and extended his open hand. "May I take a look?"

His father slammed the paper in his son's hand and shot up from his chair so fast it caused the chair to topple over. Then, he walked to the big window and stood with his back turned away from his son.

Ethan's eyes drifted to the evening paper from the day prior, and the front-page photo caused him to draw in a quick breath. *No. The Amorley Tribune*'s first page had a picture of himself and Claire standing in the Royal Gardens in an embrace. Someone had captured the photo after their Dark Forest escapade, and both of them looked disheveled. Claire had a fair amount of dirt on her clothing and sticks in her hair. It did not paint a virtuous scene. "This isn't what it looks like." He shifted his gaze toward his father.

Spinning around, his father raised a hand in the air and narrowed his eyes. "Then, please, tell me what happened. It looks like you and the successor to the Amorley Crown spent time together doing who knows what. I don't think I have to tell you that Abigail Fulton and her father are not happy about this—not at all. How many times have I said the Crown holds nothing for us?

I don't want you intermingled with that family. Abigail's family and their fortune promise more opportunities and power, but you're close to destroying that, too."

Ethan stepped closer to his father. "I'm sorry about this." He raised the offensive paper in the air. "It's not how it looks. I mean, yes, I did hug her, and we've shared a kiss, but that's it. You know I'm respectful, and my mother raised me to act like a gentleman. I wouldn't jeopardize my reputation. I'm also sorry Abigail and her family are upset by this photograph, but I'm not going to marry her."

His father rushed toward Ethan and placed both hands on his son's shoulders. He tightened his grip and spoke between clenched teeth, "Listen to me. You're going to marry Abigail. You will call her and her father today and apologize for your actions, and you will promise never to see Dr. Claire Thomson again."

Ethan met his father's gaze and raised his brow. "What if I can't do that?"

His father's eyes turned cold, and he spoke evenly, "Then, I will write you out of my will and this family. I will forbid any contact between you and your mother and ban you from the estate. And you'll lose your job." His eyes softened a bit. "Ethan, are you willing to lose everything for that girl? Is she worth it?"

Ethan didn't answer but removed himself from his father's grasp. He glanced at his mother, but she refused to meet his gaze. This was it then. He whipped around and walked out of his family's house for what might be the last time.

~

"Claire. Claire? Come here," the queen mother's

voice beckoned from the Grand Banquet Room.

Claire hurried down the hall and entered the room. Her grandmother sat at the table with Granny and Maurelle. "Yes, ma'am, did you need me?"

The queen mother furrowed her brow and raised a paper in the air. "What is this?"

She walked over to see what had caused her grandmother's concern and gasped when her eyes landed on the front page of the paper. "What is that? Who took that picture? It looks awful. It looks like we—"

The queen mother finished the sentence for her granddaughter, "It looks like you two were canoodling or worse. I don't suppose I have to tell you that part of Royal Lessons includes no canoodling, especially not in public." Her grandmother held the paper in one hand and smacked the picture with the other. "This is not discreet. This behavior is not appropriate. This is not acceptable," her voice escalated to a higher pitch with each admonishment.

Stunned, Claire searched for what to say next. "May I sit down?"

Her grandmother dropped the paper to the table and nodded. "You may. Explain yourself."

"Grandmother, it isn't what it looks like, I promise."

Granny jumped in, "It looks like he gave you a big smooch." She cackled.

Whipping her head to face Granny, Claire sent her a warning look.

Her granny grinned and shrugged. "Well it does. I can't say I blame you. He's a handsome man."

Deciding to ignore her granny, Claire faced the

queen mother again. "Grandmother, I'm so sorry. I'm telling you the truth. Ethan has been a gentleman. Yes, he kissed me, but I promise that's it. This picture," she pointed to the photograph, "was taken the day Milo went missing. If Ethan hadn't shown up at the castle and tried to find Milo and me, we'd probably have spent the night in the Dark Forest. He saved our lives."

Claire leaned closer to the picture. "I don't know how someone took this photograph. We were in the Royal Gardens at the time. It had to be taken by one of the staff or someone in the castle. Who would have given it to the press?"

The queen mother shook her head. "I cannot imagine one of our staff members doing this. It makes the Crown look bad." She sighed. "I suppose I'll have to speak with Albert about it. We must have a leak, and I cannot employ people I don't trust. I'll have him interview all of the staff and fire whoever did this."

An uncomfortable inkling tickled its way through Claire's mind. She shifted her eyes toward her stepmother. Maurelle sat at the table taking nibbles of her omelet, appearing uninterested in the conversation. However, Claire thought she noticed a small smile forming at the corner of Maurelle's lips.

"I cannot imagine who would want to hurt the Crown or me. Can you, Maurelle?"

Flicking her eyes downward at her half-eaten omelet, Maurelle set her fork down. She removed the napkin from her lap and placed it on the table before meeting Claire's gaze. "No," she replied.

Claire stared at her, hoping to see a hint of warmth so she could push the rising doubt away. Instead, her stepmother's eyes narrowed, and she rose from the table.

"Ma'am," Maurelle addressed the queen mother, "I need to attend to some matters for the gala. I shall see you later." Then, she left the room without another word to Claire.

The queen mother stood to leave as well but stopped by Claire and placed a hand on her shoulder. "I don't mean to come down so hard on you, but I don't think I have to tell you how important the Royal Gala is and the timing of the news article...well, it's less than ideal. We need the public to adore you and Parliament to submit no reason for opposition to your coronation. I realize you haven't made your mind up about taking the Throne, but I love Amorley and take the business of its future quite seriously. Please, think hard about what you want and if you are ready to commit yourself fully to this country. I'd hate to see you refuse the Crown and have it fall into unscrupulous hands, but I cannot make you choose this life."

Claire's shoulders sagged, and she nodded. "Yes, ma'am."

Her grandmother squeezed Claire's shoulder and walked away.

As Claire watched her leave, the scent of garlic and onions from the omelet mixed with the feelings of disappointment and embarrassment. Claire stamped down a wave of nausea threatening the back of her throat. She fiddled with the ends of her hair and turned her attention to Granny. "Have I let you down, too?"

Granny leaned forward in her purple top with a sequin flower broach. Through orange-colored lips, she whispered, "Honey, if you'd done anything less, I'd have been disappointed. It was worth it to see that interchange between you and old Queenie Maurelle. That woman is up to no good. I bet she's the one who leaked the photo to the press. Why, I'd say she's the one who had the photo taken. I don't trust her—not one bit. Now, let's go upstairs and regroup. You have a big day ahead filled with gala preparations."

Claire lifted a shoulder. "I guess you're right." She placed her hand on top of Granny's. "Thanks for always having my back. I love you."

Her granny winked. "You wouldn't expect anything less, would you? We Thomson girls have to stick together. I love you, too." She pressed her hands on the table, ready to rise from her seat, but paused. "Oh, I almost forgot to tell you. Albert has two messages for you. I don't know anything about them because he ran off before I could ask him, and then my stomach wouldn't stop grumbling, so I headed in here for a bite, but he told me to let you know." Then, her grandmother stood and shuffled around the table to join Claire at the kitchen door.

Claire gave Granny a hug. "I'd better find Albert. I'll meet up with you later, okay?"

Her granny kissed her on the cheek and left the room, no doubt on her way to look for more coffee—a scarce commodity around the castle. *Why did everything have to center around tea*?

Claire wandered into the kitchen and found Albert standing by the sink, teacup in hand, skimming *The Amorley Tribune*. When he noticed her presence, he flipped the paper over, so the questionable picture of her and Ethan lay face down. "Dr. Thomson, how may I help you?"

Claire's face warmed with embarrassment over the

photo, and she took a hesitant step further into the kitchen. "Uh, Granny told me you had some messages for me?"

"Yes, I do." He dug inside his jacket pocket and drew out two pieces of paper. Handing them to Claire, he met her gaze. "I'm sorry about the photograph in the paper. I assure you I had nothing to do with it, and I'm doing everything I can to find the responsible party."

Accepting the messages from Albert, Claire bobbed her head. "Thank you, Albert, for your kind words. I know it wasn't you." She glanced at the words on the papers Albert had given her. Ulrich Mendelton, Chief of Orthopedic Surgery, Halford University and her fellowship program director from Oxmund University.

Claire gulped. With only a few days left until the gala, she didn't need this reminder of her upcoming decision—her old life versus the new one. She lifted her head and sent Albert an appreciative smile. "Thanks, Albert. I'd better return these phone calls. I'm going to my room if you need me."

He nodded. "Yes, ma'am."

Claire left the kitchen and walked down the Great Hall, taking the Grand Staircase to the second floor. She walked down the hallway and entered her room. Claire closed and locked the bedroom door behind her. She fished her phone out of her purse and entered the numbers to Halford first.

A professional-sounding male voice answered the line, "Hello, this is Dr. Mendelton speaking. How may I assist you?"

Clearing her throat, Claire responded, "Um, hi, I mean, hello. This is Dr. Claire Thomson."

"Yes, Dr. Thomson, I called earlier. Unfortunately,

it concerns the matter of a photograph of you and a gentleman that surfaced in *The Amorley Tribune*."

Claire's throat tightened. "Forgive me for asking, but how do you know about that picture? I'm surprised it made its way beyond the local newspaper."

The man sighed. "The paper indicated that you might become the next queen of Amorley, Dr. Thomson. I'm surprised you're blindsided by the fact that anything and everything you do gets reported. The photo is in all of the major U.S. papers today, and it's trending on all social media. What is it the kids say today? You've gone viral."

Claire's hand flew to her forehead. Rubbing it, she tried to explain, "I'm sorry you had to see that, sir, but I assure you—"

"Dr. Thomson, I called to tell you I am rescinding our offer to you. I don't doubt the quality of your surgical and research skills. However, the university cannot have all the scrutiny and publicity that will follow you. This photo is only the beginning. I'm sorry. It's not the Halford way."

Claire's jaw ached. "I see," she whispered. "Well, if that's all, then I must be going. Thank you for considering me for—"

"Goodbye, Dr. Thomson. Have a good day." He hung up without letting her complete her sentence.

Tears filled her eyes and spilled over. Full-out sobs loomed, but she pulled in a deep breath and tried to calm herself. Claire needed to return Oxmund's call, but now she feared what they might say, too.

Wiping the tears from her eyes and cheeks with the back of her hand, Claire inhaled and exhaled slowly. After she'd settled the sobs, she pressed the numbers on the phone to Oxmund University.

Ten minutes later, she'd heard a similar story from the orthopedic fellowship head at Oxmund. He said he respected her skills and talents but didn't want to involve his institution in scandal and media frenzy. As a result, after her leave of absence expired in a few days, he expected her to remove her things from the hospital and not return.

Now, Claire permitted herself to wallow. She flung herself across her bed face down and wept until no tears remained. Her head pounding, Claire rolled over and stared at the ceiling, considering what to do next. She couldn't return to Boston to work at Halford. She couldn't stay here and finish her fellowship and practice medicine part-time at Oxmund. Medically, she had no options. Claire could accept the Crown, something she doubted she could do well, or return to the United States and start over at another medical institution. Still, it wouldn't be Halford—her dream.

Gazing at the chandelier overhead, Claire knew she should go select her gown for the Royal Gala, but she wasn't in the mood to try on dresses after the two devastating phone conversations. She heaved herself to a sitting position and sighed. As she sat on the edge of her bed, mulling over what to do with her life, someone knocked on her bedroom door. "Come in," she called.

Granny flung the door open and burst in, her eyes flashing. "You look like you've been crying. What's wrong? I thought we were trying on ball gowns or some other such nonsense today." She plopped down on the bed next to Claire and patted her granddaughter on the knee.

Lifting blurry eyes to Granny, Claire placed a hand

on top of hers. "Oh, I've made a mess of things. Halford University and Oxmund both spoke with me, and neither one of them wants me now. They saw the impending chaos after one little newspaper article and didn't want to deal with a potential royal. I'm spoiled goods—unworthy."

Her granny shook her head. "Pshaw! I won't hear you say any such thing. You're the most kind, intelligent, worthy woman I know. Those places don't deserve you. Good riddance. Now, I know something that will brighten your mood."

Raising a brow, Claire grabbed a tissue from the nightstand and blew her nose. Then, she asked, "What's that?"

Granny patted Claire on the leg and rose. "Stand up and follow me."

Staring up at the determined woman who'd help raise her, Claire debated whether to stay in her bed and wallow the rest of the day or take her grandmother's lead.

Granny waved. "Well, come on. You don't want to keep this surprise waiting."

Wiping at her tears one last time with the edge of a fresh tissue, Claire balled the tissues up and tossed them in her wastebasket. Then, she rose and followed her grandmother out of the bedroom. Claire's hair stuck to her tear-stained cheeks. She pried the strands loose and tucked them behind her ears as she walked downstairs to the Great Hall. When she arrived on the final step, Claire froze. "Ethan, what are you doing here?"

He looked handsome in a cream sweater and dark pants. His blond locks fell across his forehead into his eyes, and he ran a hand through them, pushing them back. Ethan frowned, stepped closer, and took her hand. "I had to see you. I wanted to make sure you were okay. I assume you saw the *Amorley Tribune* article?"

Claire felt terrible. This whole time she had only considered how the article affected her, but now she couldn't imagine how Ethan's family would react to open the paper and see that photo on the front page. She opened her mouth and then closed it, unsure of what to say. "Ethan, I'm sorry about the photo. I don't know who took it or how it got leaked to the press, although I have a suspicion…still, I—"

He placed his hand on her cheek and settled his thumb on her lips, silencing her apology. "You don't have to do that. It's not your fault. I came here because I wanted to make sure you were okay. I know you don't like the attention, and it did look, well, compromising. I called Michael to see if we had any legal recourse with the newspaper. He's checking on it for me. At the very least, I'll have him send them a strongly worded letter."

Claire realized her granny stood ahead of them in the Great Hall, watching the entire interchange. Ethan stood between her and Granny, so he couldn't see the kissy faces her grandmother continued to make behind his back. Sometimes, Claire felt like the grown-up in their relationship. She narrowed her eyes, staring at Granny.

Granny stopped her antics. She gave a wave and walked down the hallway, whistling as she left.

Turning her attention to Ethan again, Claire lifted her eyes to his.

He ran his hand through her hair and leaned in to give her a soft kiss on the lips.

Her heart pounded. It would be wonderful to ignore

her problems and stay like this all day, but she needed to tell him about her loss of career options since it looked like she'd have to choose the Crown or medicine. Where did love fall into all of this? She had never felt so royally confused in her life. What should she do? She took both his hands in hers and squeezed them. "I have something to tell you."

He smiled. "Sure, you can tell me anything."

She looked down at their hands before meeting his gaze again. "It's not good news. I received messages from Halford University and Oxmund University today. They both withdrew their offers of employment because of the newspaper photo. I'm not allowed to finish my fellowship. If I stay here as queen of Amorley, medicine won't be an option for me, even if Parliament approves it.

His shoulders stiffened, and his jaw went slack. "Oh. I see. Does that mean you're leaving after the gala?"

Claire looked away, and a pit formed in her stomach. How could she leave? How could she say goodbye to him and the people she'd met? She'd come to love Amorley over the past few weeks. When she looked into his eyes again, she read hurt and pain there. "I don't know. I don't know what—"

Granny came running down the hallway toward them, her arms waving in the air. Her eyes wore a look of panic. "Claire, Claire, you have…to come…quick," she panted the words out in short bursts. By the time she arrived next to Claire, she wheezed and hunched over, trying to catch her breath.

Claire placed a hand on her granny's back, trying to support her. "Calm down. What's going on?"

Granny sucked in a gulp of air and sputtered, "It's Milo—he's sick. He's really sick. It's bad."

A rock formed in Claire's stomach. "Where is he?" She glanced up and down the hallway but didn't see anyone else around.

Granny gestured behind her with her thumb. "He's out back in the Royal Garden. He's bleeding. Albert's with him. He's the one who found him."

Claire didn't wait to hear anything further. She shot off down the hall toward the back of the castle. Running as fast as possible in two-inch heels, she longed for her scrubs and tennis shoes. When arrived at the foot of the stone stairs leading to the garden, she gasped. Her hand flew to her mouth. "No!" she screamed.

Milo lay on his side on the pebbled path. Blood trickled out of his mouth and nose, and it appeared he'd vomited blood as well.

Claire sank next to him and stroked his back, trying to check his breathing.

Albert knelt next to her with blood on his hands and shirt. His hands trembled, and his eyes widened. "I'm not sure—I'm not sure what happened. The gardener sometimes uses rat poison. I suppose he could have gotten into that, although it's usually kept in the garden shed. I came out here to check on the garden staff and found him like this. I don't know how long he'd been out here or how he even got outside. Everyone knows to close the doors to the castle and keep watch for him." He looked over at Claire. "Ma'am, I'm so sorry. I'm so very sorry." Tears filled his eyes.

Seeing her stoic friend cry broke something inside of her.

Milo closed his eyes, and his breathing stopped.

A guttural cry erupted from Claire, "No. I can't lose him." She whipped her head up and searched for Ethan. He'd followed behind her with Granny in tow. Claire's medical training kicked in, and she demanded, "Ethan, you have to call a veterinarian. He needs vitamin K to reverse the anticoagulation."

Ethan and her granny stood frozen to the spot.

She shot her eyes to Albert. "You have to call someone. Why isn't anyone doing anything? We have to save him. I know we can save him." She stroked her hand down Milo's back, feeling his soft fur under her fingers. His chest didn't rise and fall. It stayed perfectly still. *No. He can't be gone. He can't.* She'd had Milo since he was a puppy, and he'd carried her through the loss of her mother, then finding out about her father and the royal debacle that ensued. If she hadn't gone looking for answers about her father and the past, then he'd still be with her. Milo would be alive.

Ethan dropped to one knee and placed a hand on Claire's shoulder. "Claire... he's gone. There aren't any veterinarians close by, so even if we took him somewhere, it would be too late."

She didn't want to hear this right now. She didn't want to hear anything. Jerking up her head, she glared at him. "If I hadn't come here to this horrible place, then Milo would still be alive. I don't know what I was thinking. I'm not good enough to be the queen of Amorley, and apparently, I'm not good enough to be a doctor at Halford. I've lost everything I cared about because I had to know who my father was and what it meant. Do you know what it meant?"

His eyes darkened, and his lips formed a tight line.

"What?"

Tears fell, and Claire sobbed. Between her cries, she whimpered, "Nothing. It all meant nothing. I wish I'd never set foot at Evercliff Castle."

Ethan stood and stared down at her. "Maybe you're right. Maybe it meant nothing." He pivoted and stormed up the stone stairs to the castle and away from her, probably for the last time.

A thick voice spoke over her left shoulder, "Oh, what a shame. Something happened to your dog, Claire?"

Claire snapped her head around and stared at her stepmother. *That's it. Of course.* Deep within her heart, she knew her stepmother was responsible for Milo's death. She didn't know how someone could be so evil, but by the haughty, pleased look on her stepmother's face, Claire knew—Queen Maurelle had killed Milo. She'd sent Claire a message—leave the castle and the Crown and never return.

Message received. Claire hissed, "You." She pointed at her stepmother. "I know you're somehow responsible for this."

Maurelle put a hand to her chest and raised her eyebrows. "Who, me? I don't see how that's possible as I know nothing about the matter. I've been busy with gala preparations. I'd say it's obvious what happened here—your rambunctious dog let his curiosity and high spirits get the best of him. He wormed his way into somewhere he didn't belong and met an unpleasant consequence."

Claire shook her head. "No, that's not what happened."

"I can't believe you'd accuse me. I've always tried

to look out for you and him. Remember? I warned you the other day when you and Ethan returned from the garden. The Dark Forest and these grounds can pose many, many hazards. I told you to be careful. Apparently, Milo didn't get the message." Maurelle swiveled and sauntered up the steps and into the castle, taking Claire's hope and joy with her.

The sky darkened overhead, and raindrops began to fall, splatting on the ground around Claire and Milo. Fitting weather. Thunder rumbled through the clouds, and a bright flash of lightning lit up the sky. The scent of rain and despair stung her nose.

Granny had followed Claire outside and now placed a hand on her shoulder. "Claire, dear... I'm sorry. I know how much he meant to you. I—"

Lifting her head to meet her granny's gaze, Claire raised a hand. "Please. Don't. I know you're trying to help, and I love you for it, but I can't hear it right now. I wish I'd never learned about my father. Then, I wouldn't have brought you and poor Milo here." She patted her furry friend's head, but he remained still and lifeless. She felt sick to her stomach.

"Don't say that—you couldn't have known. You couldn't—"

The raindrops fell heavier, quickly turning into thick sheets. Claire's hair matted against her face, and her clothes stuck to her skin. She jumped up and took off running away, anywhere, to put distance between herself and Evercliff Castle.

Water filled her shoes, and each step squished and turned her toes colder. Claire ignored the pain and pressed onward, unsure of her destination but confident she couldn't stay one minute longer looking at Milo like that.

After several minutes, her lungs ached, her thighs burned, and she slowed to a jog and then stopped. Planting her hands on her hips, she bent over at the waist, expelling all of her breakfast. When she'd emptied her stomach, she slumped to the ground, her knees tucked underneath, and wrapped her arms around herself.

The chill of the cold, damp weather caught up with her, and her teeth chattered. Still, she didn't go back. Instead, Claire opened her mouth and let all the pain, hurt, and grief of the past come out in loud, harsh sobs. She cried, "Milo, I'm sorry. I should have been there for you. I should have protected you. God, I can't do this. I can't be a queen—I can't even look after my own family. I've let my mom, father, and grandmothers down. I've ruined my career, and I've destroyed any hope of happiness with Ethan. He'll never speak to me again. Everything's a mess."

She supposed she should have asked God to help her or provide an answer, but she didn't do that—perhaps because she doubted a solution existed. She didn't deserve the help, didn't deserve love, and didn't deserve true happiness.

Claire's cries slowly subsided to short gasps until they ceased. She wiped her face, both hands pawing at her eyes, trying to remove the blurry film that wouldn't go away. With the rain still pounding down, her efforts at drying her eyes seemed futile, so she pushed to her feet and let her eyelids fall shut.

Pulling in a deep breath, she released it slowly and then turned to begin her walk back to the castle. She knew what she had to do. Dr. Claire Thomson would turn in her tiara after the Royal Gala, pack her bags, and go home.

Chapter 13
Three days until the Royal Gala

Claire spent the morning moping around her room. She stayed in her pajamas and started packing up her luggage. Claire placed each outfit selected for the trip into the suitcases. What a waste of an excursion. She'd nearly closed the lid when she remembered the picture frames on her nightstand.

Walking around the side of her bed, which held Claire's largest suitcase, she lifted the first framed photo from the side table and studied it. The picture showed Claire with her mom and Granny at the beach the summer before her mother had passed away. She traced her mother's smiling face with her fingertips, and tears filled her eyes for the thousandth time that day. *Was she doing the right thing by leaving?*

Placing the picture in her bag, Claire reached for the other one she'd brought along—a picture of her and Milo the day she'd first brought him home. His goofy grin matched her smile. They'd instantly bonded even though he stole all her socks and shredded them. A single tear fell down her cheek, but she wiped it away and shook her head. No, she had to leave. She'd only make things a bigger mess if she stayed, not to mention she'd never get to practice medicine again. If she wasn't a doctor, then what was she?

A knock sounded at the door. Claire placed the picture of her and Milo in her bag. "Come in," she called, not lifting her head.

"Hello, dear. I wondered if I might have a quick word?" the queen mother asked.

Claire turned around and nodded, then took a seat on the edge of the bed.

Her grandmother entered the room and closed the door behind her. She walked over to the bed and joined Claire, sitting down and smoothing her skirt. Placing her hands in her lap, the queen mother focused her gaze on her granddaughter. "Claire, I came to give you my condolences about Milo. I don't know how it could have happened. Still, I suppose when there are chemicals and garden supplies lying around, anything is possible."

Claire snorted. "I know who's responsible. Maurelle did it." Fresh pain stung her eyes, and she turned her head so her grandmother wouldn't see the tears.

The queen mother spoke with hesitancy, "Now, dear, we can't accuse people of things that we cannot prove. Maurelle may be difficult at times, but the Lord tells us to love our friends and our enemies, and we must believe the best about people—at least until we have reason to think otherwise."

Claire rubbed her eyes with her fingers. "You're wrong. She did it—I know she did it. I can't prove it, but she's wanted to get rid of Milo and me since we arrived. After the Royal Gala, she'll get her wish. I can't do this anymore, Grandmother. I've tried, and I've failed. She wins. Maurelle can have the throne, or my stepbrother can take it. I don't care, but it won't be me. I'll attend the gala because I promised I would go, but after it's over, I'm returning to Boston. I need to get my life back."

Placing a hand on top of her granddaughter's, the queen mother's face sagged. "I do hope you'll reconsider and change your mind. You could become a great queen. Your father would have thought so, too. Please, think about Amorley's fate if left in the hands of others."

Shaking her head, Claire murmured, "You're wrong. I'm not a queen, and as of right now, I'm not a practicing doctor. I'm nothing. No, I can't stay here. It will be better for everyone if I leave."

Her grandmother stared at her for a second. Then, she squeezed her hand before releasing it and standing. "Think about it." She walked away from Claire but paused at the door. Looking over her shoulder, she caught Claire's gaze. "One more thing, will you have an escort for the gala? I know Granny will attend, but I didn't know if I should add anyone else to the guest list."

With a firm shake of the head, Claire replied, "No," and stood, busying herself with packing her last few sweaters. She zipped the suitcase shut and waited for her grandmother to leave.

Before the door clicked closed, the queen mother spoke softly, "I almost forgot—I wanted you to wear something special for the gala. It's my first tiara. I wore it on my first day as queen. I believe you'll find it on the display hutch in Maurelle's study. I let her use it for her wedding day when she married your father and told her she could place it there as a memento."

Claire's jaw clenched, and she whipped around.

"Grandmother, you cannot expect me to go into Maurelle's personal space. If she found me there, she'd have a fit." She thought about Milo's fate. "Or worse."

Her grandmother persisted, "It's not her decision. The tiara still belongs to me, and I want you to have it. Besides, she's out riding right now. She won't even know you've gone in there, and it's not hers to miss." With this final decree, the queen mother left, closing the door behind her.

Wonderful. Claire had to face a crowded room wearing fancy dress-up clothes and give a speech turning down the Crown in a few days. Now, she also had to undertake a secret mission into enemy territory—Maurelle's study. Claire disagreed with her grandmother. If her stepmother found Claire in her study taking the tiara, Maurelle would care. A lot.

Claire sighed, stood, adjusted her jeans, and zipped up her hooded sweatshirt. She looked very unroyal today, but she didn't care. Slipping her feet into her familiar white clogs, she trudged out the room and down the hallway to the smaller study claimed by Maurelle.

As she entered the room, Claire drew in a deep breath. It looked different than the rest of the castle— darker. Emerald tapestries pulled shut blocked out the sunlight from a large window across the room. One side of the room held a bookshelf encompassing the entire wall, its shelves filled with books. She puckered her nose from the musty smell. Usually, Claire loved reading, but the scent of the study carried a foreboding odor. She shuddered.

Stepping further into the room, Claire noted a large mirror hung on the wall at the other end of the room. It sat above a black writing desk with a wingback chair in front of it. The only light in the room came from an open transom above the space's main window.

Claire walked further into the room and headed for the desk. She pulled the wingback chair out and sat down. Glancing over her shoulder, Claire listened for her stepmother's footsteps coming down the hall and held her breath. After a second of silence, she released the breath and began her assignment.

She looked down at the desk and saw the drawer slightly ajar. Various letters and pieces of paper lay inside, but she tried to focus on retrieving the tiara so she could get out of Maurelle's room quickly.

Claire scanned the hutch attached to the desk, her eyes landing on a beautiful crown inside a glass box on the second shelf. She half-stood and leaned forward to retrieve the tiara but jostled the desk drawer in doing so. It made a thud and her heart stopped. *Oh no! Now she'd broken the desk.*

She grabbed the tiara and placed it on top of the desk before bending down to see what damage she'd done. The underside of the desk drawer hung down. *What?* The desk had a false bottom. *How strange.*

Poking at it, she tried to encourage it back to its previous place, but the drawer sunk back down. This time, though, an envelope fell to the ground. She picked it up and turned it over, not intending to read the address, but her gaze settled on the name, and she froze. *Dr. Claire Thomson.* The letter bore her name and address in Boston.

Claire flipped the envelope over, but the other side remained bare. *Should she open it?* Technically, it had her name on it. She debated her decision for two seconds longer, then tore open the top of the envelope.

Pulling out the letter, she skimmed the words and noted the return address at the top:

Alexander Isaac Evercliff, King of Amorley
Evercliff Castle
1 Royal Lane
Dorekshire, Amorley 22244

Claire's hand flew to her lips. Her father had written her a letter. *Why hadn't he sent it?*

She knew she should take it with her and read it in her room, but Claire didn't think she could wait another minute to find out what it said. Placing it on the desk, she smoothed out its creases and closed her eyes. Could she handle knowing what her father had written to her? Still uncertain, curiosity defeated self-doubt, and she opened her eyes and started reading.

Dearest Claire,

> *I don't know where to begin. Your mother, Mona, wrote to me a month ago, and I've been trying to summon the courage to contact you. She apologized to me for keeping your existence a secret and said she'd only done so to protect you from the scrutiny and expectations of royal life. I cannot say I entirely blame her, though I grieve the lost time with you.*

> *Mona told me she is sick and that her cancer is terminal. I'm so sorry that you will lose your mother. When I think of my time with her, I consider myself truly blessed. She brought light, energy, and laughter into my life. I wish I'd been able to convince her to stay in our marriage. Still, I understood then as I do now*

the struggles and pressures royal life and my father's opinions would have placed upon her.

Your mother came to Amorley to study at Oxmund University. She stayed for a year, and during the first month of her trip, I met her at the Amorley Foundation Art Gallery. I stood across the room staring at this beautiful, blonde woman who seemed fascinated with each piece, and while she studied the art, I studied her. I couldn't take my eyes off of her.

I introduced myself, and she amazed me with her grace and intelligence. We began dating and fell in love, and a few weeks before she planned to return to the United States, we married in secret. When my father discovered our union, he became furious. Your mother's commoner status and the rushed relationship angered and concerned him. He said Parliament would not approve the marriage, and neither did he.

My father gave me an ultimatum—the Crown or your mother—and I had prepared to choose Mona. However, she knew how much Amorley and its people meant to me and did not want to live under the microscope of palace life, so she chose for me and left. One week after she left, she sent me annulment papers, and the entire matter was kept quiet. Otherwise, I never heard from her again.

Your mother said she found out about her pregnancy after she'd left Amorley and didn't want to burden me with a scandal or saddle you with the public scrutiny. She kept you and your royal bloodline a secret.

I've considered how not having a father must have felt for you. I imagine you must have thought I'd abandoned you or didn't want you—that is not true. Had I known about you, Claire, I would have crossed the ocean to beg your mother to return to me. I would have loved you both with all of my heart.

Mona told me about your medical accomplishments, and I want you to know I'm so proud of you. I understand that to you I'm a stranger, but I hope to become more than that. I pray, Claire, that you might let me get to know you and someday become what I should have been all those years ago—your father.

In closing, I want to share something God placed in my heart as I considered what to say to you. You are chosen, you are wanted, and you have a father who loves you. I pray this letter finds you well and that when you are ready to talk or meet, you will let me know. I included the palace contact number at the bottom of the letter along with a verse I want to leave with you. I love you, Claire, and I'm sorry for the mess your mother and I made of the past, but I know the future holds the promise of possibility.

I'm praying for your mother, too. Please let me know if I can do anything for you or her.

God bless you,

Alexander Evercliff (Dad)

> *P.S. I found this verse and wanted to share it with you. "But you are a chosen people, a royal priesthood, a holy nation, God's special possession, that you may declare the praises of him who called you out of darkness into his wonderful light." 1 Peter 2:9.*

Her father had wanted her. He loved her, and he'd hoped to make a new start with her by way of the letter. One thought still nagged her. *Why had the letter remained hidden in the underside of a desk drawer?* Realization settled upon Claire—Maurelle must have found the letter after he wrote it. Maybe she offered to mail it and intercepted it somehow. Even though she couldn't prove it, Claire knew her stepmother hadn't wanted her father to meet his long-lost daughter. *Of course.* It would have meant that her son wouldn't rule, and she'd lose her chance at ultimate power.

She'd lost her opportunity to meet her father. Staring at the letter in her hand, Claire saw a tear fall onto it, creating a blurred spot in the ink. More tears followed, and she let the release of a good cry take over. After several minutes, her weeping subsided, and she folded the letter again, returning it to the envelope. She shoved it inside her pants pocket and tried to push the bottom of the desk drawer into place. Three attempts later, it seemed to hold, and Claire wiped her face off with the edge of her sleeve and rose from the chair. Grabbing the tiara from the desktop, she surveyed the room to make sure it looked as she'd found it.

Confident she'd left no trace, Claire hurried out of the room and down the hallway to the safety of her bedroom. She opened her door and rushed through it, quietly closing it behind her. Then, she leaned her back against it and slid to the floor. Pulling the letter out of her pocket, she opened it, reading it once more. Her father loved her, and he'd reminded her how much God loved her, too. He'd said she was worthy and hoped she would rule Amorley someday.

Now that Claire had read the truth, she knew what she had to do—she had to take her place as the queen of Amorley, but she would do it on her own terms. Claire didn't know how she would convince everyone to let her practice medicine and take the Crown, but she wouldn't stop until she found a solution.

Claire prayed God would help her fix things with Ethan. She had to tell him how much he meant to her. Whether he still cared for her or not, God valued her, and that mattered most. Still, her heart yearned for Ethan, and she suspected if she didn't tell him, she'd always regret it.

Then, her thoughts turned to Milo. She couldn't undo the loss of him, but Claire wouldn't let her stepmother win. After gazing at the letter for a few minutes more, she folded it, looked at her packed-up room, and stood to her feet again. If she hoped to slay a dragon, she'd need help, and one person came to mind.

Chapter 14
Two days until the Royal Gala

Ethan couldn't believe how things had ended between himself and Claire. The day before had felt surreal. After their argument, he'd climbed in his car and left the castle, driving away with no destination. Without realizing it, he found himself pulling into a parking space in front of the townhouse of his friend, Michael. He had turned off the car and hopped out, unsure of what hope or answers Michael could provide. But finding a way for Claire to stay would make the first step toward fixing the mess he'd made.

He didn't know why he'd fought with her and stormed away. That's not true—he knew why. He'd let his pride and hurt feelings get between him and the first person he'd truly loved. Ethan pressed the doorbell and waited.

Michael opened the door and raised a brow. "Hey, Ethan, what's going on? We didn't have plans for today, did we?"

Ethan ignored the question and pressed on with his own, "Can I come in?"

Furrowing his brow, Michael swung the door further. "Sure. Is everything okay?"

Ethan pushed past his friend and entered the

brick townhouse. He crossed the foyer and planted himself in a formal chair in the sitting room.

Michael followed his friend into the room and with a confused expression sat down in a chair across from him. He started to open his mouth but closed it before speaking.

Ethan filled the silence with a question, "Did you make any headway with Claire's problem? About her accepting the Crown but still retaining the ability to pursue medical endeavors?"

Michaels' eyes widened. "Were you listening in on my conversation this morning?"

Shaking his head, Ethan replied, "No. Why?"

Michael pulled a piece of paper from inside his jacket pocket and opened it. "I got off the phone with a friend from the Historical Committee. He knows every facet of the constitution and bylaws, and if anyone might find a loophole for your friend, then he could do it."

Ethan leaned forward, resting his elbows on his knees and clasping his hands together as if praying. "And?"

Smiling, Michael shifted his gaze to the paper in his hand and continued, "And the good news is, he found one—a big one. An article at the end of the constitution states that despite Parliament having the power to approve the future ruler of Amorley, Parliament does not carry full veto power to deny an appointment. The constitution states, 'The acting ruler of the land shall determine the heir apparent.' In this case, that person is the queen mother. She holds the power to name Claire or whomever she deems fit to rule. However, the constitution's next few lines indicate that precedence has always been that the eldest blood relative takes the throne—which again would be Claire. Parliament cannot deny the appointment, save for an accusation of treason." Michael looked at his notes and then moved his gaze to Ethan. "She hasn't done anything treasonous, has she?"

Ethan sent his friend a small smile. "No, not that I know of."

Michael nodded. "Good." Then, he glanced at his notes again. "The constitution does require the queen or king of Amorley to devote their loyalty to the Crown. It does not forbid other endeavors as long as those activities do not harm the state of affairs of Amorley or its people." Michael peered at Ethan again. "I cannot imagine that helping patients a few times a month would harm Amorley or its people. Can you?"

Ethan's grin widened. "No, I can't. Michael, thank you. I can't wait to tell Claire except—" He recalled she might not be thrilled to hear from him based on their most recent interaction.

Michael raised his forehead. "What?"

Frowning, Ethan rose and headed over to the large window that looked out onto the busy street below. Cars passed in both directions, and a couple strolled along the sidewalk hand in hand. They made it look so easy—holding hands, laughing, as if being in love were simple. He'd felt like that, too. Loving Claire had seemed as easy as breathing. He had to win her back. Ethan didn't know if she'd listen to him, but for Amorley's sake and Claire's, he had to try. He needed her to know what Michael had shared with him.

Ethan thought about Milo, and his shoulders sagged. Milo had meant so much to Claire. She must feel devastated. What could he do about that? He couldn't bring her dog back. No, but he wouldn't let Queen Maurelle succeed. She'd been behind every awful thing that had come Claire's way since her arrival in Amorley. That all stopped now. He would raise his sword and slay any dragons that came between Claire and her happiness. She was the most wonderful, beautiful woman he'd ever known, and he intended to do everything in his power to make her feel loved and worthy.

~

Claire had asked Granny to take a walk with her after she'd tended to Milo. Thankfully, Albert had helped Claire clean him up and find a beautiful spot under an oak tree to bury him. Albert said he'd seen him digging at the base of the tree and chasing squirrels there, so he thought Milo would have been pleased with the location of his final resting place.

Claire sank to her knees next to the burial plot and hung her head. "Milo, thank you for all the joy and happiness you brought into my life. Thanks for loving me unconditionally and for making the dark days look brighter. I'll miss you, buddy." Her eyes stung, and she wept.

The sky had been overcast that morning, but as her sobbing subsided, the clouds began to part. Claire felt a gentle hand rest on her back, and she lifted her head and turned around.

"Come take a walk with me. Let's talk." Granny didn't leave any other option than for Claire to obey, so she rose from her spot on the ground and dusted off her pants.

She followed her granny away from Milo's tree,

and the sun peeked through the clouds, warming Claire's face. Sadness over the loss of Milo lingered, and she suspected she'd carry the pain of losing him for years to come. He'd filled a hole in her heart after her mother's passing, and now, that space gaped open wide. Still, with the sun shining on her face, Claire felt a tiny promise of hope for the future. She couldn't undo the past or shy away from her grief, but she could step forward knowing her identity—a princess of the King, a child of God, a loved daughter and granddaughter.

Granny glanced at Claire and took her hand as they walked down the Royal Garden's pebbled pathway. "I have a proposition for you."

Claire raised her brow. "Oh?"

"Yes. I say you give it a go here in Amorley. I think you should take the Crown, lead like nobody's business, save these people from old Queenie and her son, and find that handsome young man and smooth things over with him."

Claire chuckled. "Oh, is that all I have to do?"

Granny nodded. "That's it. Simple. Where do we start?"

The pair continued down the path, approaching the rear entrance of the castle. Claire hooked her arm in her granny's and shrugged. "I suppose I need a good acceptance speech and gown for the gala. I wonder if I should let the queen mother know of our plans?"

Granny shook her head. "Don't say a word to anyone inside those castle walls. I think Maurelle has the place bugged."

Claire laughed but wondered about the truth of Granny's statement. "Good point. Okay, so I'll make the acceptance of the Crown a surprise. What about

Oxmund University? I don't see how I'm going to practice medicine here if the premier academic and surgical center thinks I'm a publicity risk."

Granny stopped walking and put her hands on her hips. "Don't tell me you're going to let a little picture in a newspaper stop you. Call Oxmund and ask for a second chance. People give them and receive them all the time. I don't see why they can't extend one to you. You'll never know if you don't try."

Claire digested her granny's advice and smiled. "Okay. Maybe you're right. It can't hurt to ask."

Granny grinned and gave a firm nod. "Exactly." She continued her way toward the castle with her arm still linked to Claire.

Staring at her feet as she walked, Claire ran through a list of things to do before the gala. "What about a gown? I don't have much time to select something."

"That's easy. We'll look through the gowns Albert brought to your room the other day, pick one, decide on your shoes, and then your outfit is done. Check. "

Claire raised a brow. "What will you wear? You haven't had time to shop."

Granny gave her a quick wink. "Honey, I look good in everything." She cackled, then patted her granddaughter's hand. "Don't worry about me. I brought plenty of sequined tops with me, enough to last the summer. I'll figure out something. Besides, I don't want to outshine the future queen of Amorley," she donned an aristocratic accent.

"You're silly." Then, Claire became serious. "Thanks for helping me. I don't think I could do this without you."

"No problem. Now, we'd better get shaking if

you're going to get all this done in two days."

Claire sent her granny a grateful smile, but her thoughts returned to Ethan and the way they'd left things.

"Now, what's that frown about?" Granny stopped at the base of the steps before they entered the castle.

Claire shook her head. "Oh, I wish things hadn't fallen apart with Ethan. I guess you'll have to escort me to the Royal Gala."

Giving her granddaughter's hand one final pat, Granny nodded. "I'd be honored, but don't count Ethan out of the running yet." Then, she walked arm in arm with Claire up the stairs to Evercliff Castle whistling an upbeat tune.

Grinning, Claire pondered how much had changed, but it made her smile to know that some things remained the same. Thanks to her father's letter and Granny's encouragement, Claire believed she'd never doubt her worth again.

~

The past day felt like a whirlwind of trying on dresses, shoes, and different hairstyles. After settling on her "look" for the Royal Gala, Claire turned her attention to her next task: calling Oxmund. *Ugh.* Even though Claire's letter from her father had boosted her self-confidence and made her see how much God loved her, she still worried that Oxmund might not view her in the same light. She suspected they looked at her like a communicable disease.

Picking up the phone and entering the number to the orthopedic chair's office, Claire drew in a breath and closed her eyes. As the phone rang, she released it.

"Good afternoon, this is the office of orthopedics,

Oxmund University. How may I assist you?" a secretary's voice greeted her.

Claire opened her eyes and summoned the courage she'd mustered over the past day. "Yes, this is Dr. Claire Thomson. I would like to speak with Dr. Wexford, please."

Silence answered Claire.

Pacing her bedroom floor, Claire pressed on, "Hello? Hello? Did you hear me, ma'am?"

The secretary finally responded, "Yes, Dr. Thomson. I know who you are. Everyone in Amorley knows who you are by now. Just a moment. Dr. Wexford has a busy day. Let me see if he can take a moment to speak to you."

The line went quiet, and Claire used the void to whisper a quick prayer for the Chair to give her a second chance.

"Hello? Dr. Thomson, I'm surprised to hear from you again. I thought when we spoke the other day that I made myself—"

Cutting him off before he could squelch her dreams, Claire dove into her plea, "Dr. Wexford, I'm calling to ask for another chance. I realize having me at your institution draws a great deal of publicity to Oxmund. I also know some of that publicity recently hasn't been good."

He sputtered, "I should say not. At Oxmund, we pride ourselves on maintaining a certain image, and—"

She didn't give him a chance to finish. "I know, and believe me, I want to contribute to that image, not tarnish it. I promise what you saw in the newspapers the other day does not reflect the person I am or hope to become as queen of Amorley. Please, hear me out."

Dr. Wexford grumbled but acquiesced, "Very well."

Pulling in another gulp of air, Claire stopped pacing and stood still. "Recently, I've learned more about who I am and where I come from, and it's taught me something important. I have to believe I'm worthy of the good things in my life and that what I do beyond medicine is enough. That might not make a lot of sense to you, but trust me, it's changed my perspective. Coming to Amorley and finding out about my father and his royal life showed me that I'm wanted and needed here. The people of Amorley need me, the queen mother needs me, and I think Oxmund University needs me. I know the details of my working at Oxmund may pose a challenge to coordinate. Also, I'll bring a certain amount of public scrutiny to the university, but not all publicity is bad. I can give patients excellent care, continue to practice medicine part-time, and establish a charity in conjunction with the Crown for underserved communities."

He considered her argument for a few seconds. "Hmm. A charitable fund, you say. Tied directly between Oxmund and the Crown?"

She nodded even though he couldn't see her. "Yes. I think that would look wonderful for the university, and patients would benefit from it. I could go to fundraising functions to encourage donations and speak on behalf of the university. I assure you I'll be more careful in the future about who gets close to me—no more scandalous photos in the papers."

He only murmured, "Hmm."

"Please, sir. I know I can do a good job. This country and your institution need me—as much I need them."

"Okay. We can do a trial basis. I know you could become the future queen of Amorley. However, I have to maintain the medical integrity of this facility. I expect a lot of my staff, but I'm sure we can work something out in terms of scheduling—and don't forget your promise of the charity."

Excitement bubbled up in Claire's stomach, and she did a little jig in the middle of her bedroom. "I won't, sir. Thank you so much. Thank you."

"Yes, yes. Well, I do have to go now. I have a slew of meetings this afternoon, and I—"

She stopped dancing. "One more thing, sir—if you don't mind."

"What's that?"

In all her excitement about securing a medical job, she forgotten that he would know her intentions to stay in Amorley. She did not want Maurelle or anyone else to know besides Granny—yet. "Sir, would you keep this information to yourself? I'm supposed to declare my plans regarding the Crown at the Royal Gala, and I don't want the word getting out prematurely. Do you understand?"

He cleared his throat. "Absolutely. The last thing I want is a tacky article and speculation. Let's wait until the Royal Gala to have the announcement about Oxmund made."

"Oh, I have a wonderful idea. Why don't you attend the Gala as my guest? Then, we can take a nice photo at the end of the evening for the paper declaring our plans."

"That would be fine. Now, if there's nothing else…"

"No, thank you again. I'll put your name on the list

and see you there. Have a good day, sir."

"You, too." Then, he ended the call.

Claire turned off her phone, walked to her bed, and sank on it. Setting her phone down next to her, she said a quick prayer of thanks, her hands shaking from excitement. *Things might work out after all.* She still didn't know how she'd repair her relationship with Ethan or if he'd even attend the gala, much less speak to her. Still, for now, she felt encouraged by the promise of Oxmund and the Crown working together. Maybe she could have it all. *Maybe.*

As she bathed in the happiness of hope about the future, a troubling thought tickled her brain. *Granny.* What would she do about Granny? She couldn't ask her to leave her entire life behind in Boston. Granny had lots of friends and activities she enjoyed. How could she request her to upend everything and move to Evercliff? At the same time, Claire couldn't imagine rarely seeing her granny. Since her mother's passing, Granny and Milo had been Claire's family. Now that Milo was gone, Claire didn't know if she could give up Granny, too.

She sat contemplating her choice when Granny burst into the room without knocking.

Claire jumped, startled by the sudden intrusion. "You nearly gave me a heart attack. What's going on?"

Granny clasped her hands together and looked like she'd beat Old Lady Pearl at Bingo. "I have the best news! I—" She noticed Claire sitting on the bed wearing a frown. "Hey, why are you so sad? I thought we were storming the castle—taking the Crown, claiming victory over Maurelle. What's there to get you down besides the issue with Ethan? Oh, that's what I wanted to tell you."

Claire caught her granny's gaze. "It's not that. In all the excitement about the plans you and I made, I forgot something."

Walking over, Granny sat down on the edge of the bed beside her granddaughter. She looked into Claire's eyes and furrowed her brow. "What?"

"I can't ask you to move here permanently. How can I do that? Make you give up your entire life? It's not fair to you. But I don't want to live apart from you, either. You're my family." Claire turned her attention to her lap and started picking at her fingernail.

Placing a hand on top of Claire's to stop her fiddling, Granny tipped her head, forcing Claire to meet her eyes. "Claire, my dear, sweet Claire, don't you know?"

"Know what?"

"That you are my life. Ever since the day you were born, you've brought me nothing but joy. Don't think for a minute I'm letting you move across the world without me. It looks like I'm extending my trip— indefinitely." She chuckled.

Claire shook her head. "I can't ask you to do that. What about your house in Boston? What about your friends?"

Granny waved off these concerns. "Don't worry about any of that. I'll sell the house. You may have to help me move, but I'm staying with you. The way I see it, you need an extra set of eyes to watch your back. We can't let old Queenie win. Who says you and I can't lay roots down here? Darkness cannot stand where light resides. I read that once on the back of a pamphlet, but it's true—and you're the light in this situation. It's not as easy being queen as it looks. People may always try to knock you off your throne, just like in my soaps back home on the television. The only thing is—we're going to have to introduce these people to bingo."

Claire laughed and threw her arms around her grandmother. "Thank you. You're the best. I love you."

Her grandmother squeezed her and whispered, "I love you, too." She released Claire, and her smile widened. "Now, for the best news."

Claire lifted her brow. "What's the best news?"

"I called Ethan's office and spoke with his secretary today. Left him a message. I said to tell him he'd be a fool to let you go, and that if he had any courage and sense at all in that handsome head of his, he'd come to the Royal Gala and talk with you."

Claire drew in a sharp breath. "What did she say?" After the way she'd spoken to Ethan the other day, she wouldn't blame him if he didn't want to see her again.

"His secretary said she would give him the message." Her granny looked pleased with herself.

Claire didn't see that Granny had made much progress. Her smile faded. "Oh. Okay. Thanks." She didn't want her granny to feel like she'd failed at her mission, so she forced her smile back into place.

Granny gave her hand another squeeze. "We'd better get some sleep. Tomorrow's a big day." Then, she rose from her seat and walked to the door. She turned before leaving and blew Claire a kiss like she'd done every night when Claire's mother had worked, and she'd had the task of putting Claire to bed. "Goodnight. Sweet dreams."

Claire lifted a hand and pressed it to her lips, sending her granny a kiss in return. "Goodnight."

Closing the door behind her, Granny left the room.

The words lingered in the air. *Sweet dreams. Yeah, right.* She had a lot on her mind. *What if Ethan didn't even come to the gala?* He might have decided she wasn't worth the trouble and turned his attention to Abigail to please his father and simplify his life.

Claire readied herself for bed, changing into pajamas and settling under the covers. As she pulled the blanket to her chin and closed her eyes, Claire imagined herself in the Grand Ballroom, dancing with Ethan, a tiara on her head and a stethoscope around her neck. Maybe she could have it all. The idea both puzzled and amused her, and as she fell asleep, she thought perhaps tonight's dreams would be sweet.

Chapter 15
The Day of the Royal Gala

Ethan awoke thinking that today would have been a wonderful celebration for himself and Claire if things hadn't fallen apart. He debated whether to hole up in his townhouse all day or head into work. His father left him a message the day prior, demanding Ethan attend the gala with Abigail. Since Ethan didn't know if he could avoid his father or Abigail at the Kane Estate or his apartment, he decided to take his chances at the office.

As he headed to his car, his phone rang. His secretary's name flashed across the screen. Pressing the green button, he answered, "Hello, Katherine. I'm on my way to the office now."

Katherine typed on a keyboard in the background. "Oh, I didn't know if I should expect you today. Thought you might need the day to get ready for the Royal Gala tonight. I assumed with your family's connections you planned to attend."

He opened his car door and slid inside the SUV. "I don't think I'm going tonight, Katherine. What can I do for you?" Turning the ignition, he pulled out of the driveway and navigated through the early morning traffic.

"I received a message for you yesterday, and I meant to give it to you at the end of the day. That last appointment took so long, and I got caught on the phone with another call, and I apologize, sir, but I forgot to pass the message on to you."

The sun shone overhead, and Ethan flipped the visor down to shield his eyes. Annoyed at the brightness, he curtly asked, "Who called?"

He could hear her rustling some papers before she answered, "A Mrs. Margaret Thomson called. She said she needed to speak with you, and the matter was of great importance. Those weren't her words. I believe the actual phrasing went something like, 'If you had any sense in your handsome head, you'd call her back.'"

The sun, which had aggravated him seconds before, now warmed Ethan with hope. He chuckled. "I can hear her saying something like that. Thanks, Katherine. I'll call her back." Then, he ended the call with the press of a button on his steering wheel. He pulled out of traffic and parked on the side of the road, entering the number Katherine had given him to reach Claire's granny.

Her rough voice answered, "It's about time you called me back. I'd almost given up on you. I thought, if that boy doesn't call me back and fight for my granddaughter, I'll bop him on the head. It's a good thing you showed some sense."

He smiled. "Thanks, Mrs. Thomson. I'm sorry it took so long for me to return your call, but my secretary just gave me the message moments ago. What's this about?"

Granny snorted. "What do you think? Hmm? It's about that lovely granddaughter of mine. Are you going to let her go so easily?"

"Well, I—"

Margaret Thomson pressed on, "I mean, love doesn't come around every day, you know, and my granddaughter is a catch. Besides being a doctor and beautiful, she's going to become the next queen of Amorley. Who wouldn't want a chance with her?"

He ran a hand through his hair, trying to explain, "No, you're right, but I don't know—"

"I know you don't know. You don't know anything, so I'll tell you. Claire loves you. She wants to stay in Amorley and take the Crown. Since Parliament can't stop her from pursuing her medical interests, she can do both. Part-time, of course. I'm sure ruling a country is time-consuming, but she's always been an excellent multitasker. You should have seen her handle medical school and a job, I—"

Ethan felt a smile forming. "What do you mean? She's going to stay? I thought Halford and Oxmund refused to take her. I thought she'd planned to return home to the United States and start over. I thought she didn't care about me—"

"Well, you thought wrong. Claire called Oxmund yesterday and worked things out with some big shot at the university, and she's going to accept her birthright of the Crown tonight. Of course, coronation won't be for a while. Still, I guess the queen mother said midnight tonight posed some deadline, and if Claire doesn't publicly announce her acceptance by then, well, Maurelle and her son could step forward and take over. I don't think anyone in Amorley wants that. Do you?"

He shook his head, grinning. "No, ma'am, I don't." His smile faltered a bit. "Why didn't Claire tell me herself?"

"Oh, that girl. She's hardheaded—always has been. She loves you—she told me so. I think she's afraid that you wouldn't talk to her. I told her things have a way of working out. So, I'm working it out. Call me your fairy godmother—or hers. Either way, you need to be at the gala tonight by nine p.m. She plans to make her announcement by eleven, and I want her to have you by her side. What's it going to be?"

Ethan's heart pounded harder, and he knew the answer before it formed on his lips, "I'll be there. Nine o'clock p.m."

"Good, and don't be late. Also, don't tell anyone about this. Claire and I don't trust old Queenie Maurelle, so we want to keep Claire's intentions a secret until she makes her speech. Oh, and that's another matter. She's not the greatest speech-giver, in case you hadn't noticed. Say a little prayer for her."

Ethan recalled the microphone's fate at the polo match. Nodding, he smiled. "Will do. Can I ask you something?"

"Sure, but then I've got to go—lots to do before tonight. At my age, it takes me a little longer to get ready for a shindig. Oh, who am I kidding? It takes a lot longer."

"I'll be quick. How is Claire handling losing Milo?"

Claire's granny sighed. "Not good. Not good at all. He and I were her only family. She's broken up about it."

Ethan's throat tightened. He hated to imagine Claire in pain. Of course, she'd feel upset after losing a best friend. "I'm sorry to hear it." At that moment, he knew what to do. "I'll see you tonight. I'll be on time, and I won't say a word to anyone."

"Okay, young man, don't let me down." Granny hung up the call, leaving him in silence.

Glancing at the clock on the dash of his car, Ethan realized he didn't have a lot of time. He started the engine and slipped into the steady stream of traffic, this time heading toward the shopping district to grab a few things for the gala. As he drove, the sun shone brighter, and for the first time in days, his heart soared. He couldn't wait to see Claire tonight and tell her how he felt—that he loved her and wanted to spend the rest of his life with her.

~

Claire smoothed out a wrinkle in the skirt of her sapphire ball gown and inspected her reflection. *Not bad.* She still didn't feel entirely comfortable seeing a tiara on top of her head, but she supposed in time she'd get used to it. As a little girl, she'd not been the type to dream of becoming a princess one day. No, she felt more at home in scrubs and a stethoscope. Since that outfit didn't pass Albert's or the queen mother's attire expectations for the evening, she'd settled on the blue dress and the shortest heels available.

Claire walked out of the bedroom and took the stairs down to the castle's main floor.

Granny awaited her at the bottom and gave a low whistle. "You look outstanding. There won't be another gal in that ballroom prettier than you."

Heat filled Claire's face. "Thanks. I don't know if that's true, but I'll take the encouragement." Recalling the speech that she had to make in less than an hour caused her stomach to clench. "I'm nervous. What if I make a fool of myself tonight? Remember how well the opening remarks at the polo match went?"

Granny waved off her concern. "Nonsense. You'll do fine. Just remember, you're going to become the queen. The Amorley people seem to love you, especially after you helped that young man at the polo match. If you become overwhelmed, find my face in the crowd. I'll send you a wink." Then, she gave Claire a wink for good measure.

Claire laughed. "Okay, it's a plan."

The queen mother approached Claire and took a place at her side. "Hello, dear. You look lovely. Are you ready for tonight? I hope you have good news to share with all of us."

Claire didn't want to say too much for fear that Maurelle would find out and intervene, but she didn't want to cause the queen mother concern. "I think you'll be pleased, but I don't want to say anything official until it's time for my speech."

The queen mother sent her a smile and nodded. "That makes me happy. Don't forget—you must give your speech at eleven p.m. Midnight is the deadline for publicly declaring that you've accepted your place as heir to the throne. I don't want to cut our time close. The last thing we need is to hand the Crown over to Maurelle based on a technicality. Which reminds me…"

Claire raised a brow. "What?"

Her grandmother placed a gloved hand on Claire's cheek. "Your final Royal Lesson is this—you are worthy and loved, just as you are." Then, she clasped Claire's hands in hers.

Claire nodded. "Thank you, Grandmother. I

promise I'll be on time for the speech." As she spoke to her grandmothers, one of Maurelle's assistants walked past her. Claire had seen the assistant around the castle, but the young man had seemed to vanish after Milo's death. It surprised her to see him here tonight. Claire clamped her mouth shut and sent a warning look to Granny and the queen mother, raising a finger to her lips.

The queen mother nodded. "Well, since things seem sorted here, I'll take my leave. Oh, before I go, I wondered…will I see the Earl of Abbingdon tonight?"

Claire's mouth turned downward, and she shrugged. "I don't know. Granny won't say a word about him." She turned to look at Granny.

Granny sent Claire and the queen mother a tight-lipped shake of the head. "You need to have a little faith in people, Claire," Granny chastised. "Now, I'm off to see if I can grab one of those jumbo shrimps I saw go past while you jabbered. I'll find you in a few minutes." Then, she scurried away on a quest for food.

The queen mother left as well, leaving Claire alone. She entered the Grand Ballroom, not sure what to expect. Her grandmother had told her that Albert would announce the royal family around nine p.m., and a glance at the large clock on the Grand Ballroom wall showed five minutes to spare.

She smiled and chatted with a few guests, scanning the room for Ethan. Her smile faded a bit when she didn't see his face in the crowd. Claire rallied her emotions as she walked to the front of the room for the Royal Introduction. All she had to do for this part of the evening was walk across a stage, smile, wave, and cross to the other side. As long as she didn't trip and fall down the two sets of stairs, she would be fine. *Easy.*

As Claire approached the stage, she felt someone's gaze upon her. Lifting her head, she caught Maurelle's wicked grin from the corner of her eye. She turned to look at her stepmother, and Maurelle's eyes narrowed. Claire didn't know whether to ignore Maurelle or paste a fake smile on her face and acknowledge the queen's presence. Instead, she turned her head toward the stage and focused on not tripping.

Taking each stair one at a time, Claire raised her skirt with both hands, trying not to catch the hem on her heel. At the top step, she paused and waited to hear her name called.

At the stage's center stood Albert with a microphone, dressed in a tuxedo with tails. He brought the microphone closer to his lips. "Presenting this evening hostess, the queen mother of Amorley."

Claire's grandmother glided across the stage and paused in the center. She waited for the applause to quiet before continuing to the other side.

Claire gulped. *No turning back now.*

Albert darted his eyes toward Claire and sent her a small smile of encouragement. "Presenting, Dr. Claire Thomson, granddaughter of the queen mother of Amorley."

Claire swallowed hard and placed one foot forward. She focused on her gait and tried to block out the sound of clapping in the background. Stopping in the middle of the stage, she faced the audience and did a small curtsy as her grandmother had taught her during their Royal Lessons.

The audience's applause grew, and before she grew lightheaded from the attention, Claire moved across the stage. Arriving at the other side, she then made her way down the stairs without incident and exhaled. *One obstacle overcome.* Claire released her skirt and shook out her hands.

A voice purred in her ear, "Nervous, my dear?"

Claire spun around. *Maurelle.* Claire's palms grew clammy, but she answered, "Not particularly. Why do you ask?"

Maurelle gave a sharp nod toward Claire's hands. "I thought it looked like you were shaking, but I must have been mistaken."

Claire clasped her hands together to steady them. "No, I'm fine. Thank you."

Nodding, Maurelle started to turn away but paused. She glanced at Claire and smiled. "I wonder, might I have a word with you in the library? I found something that belonged to your father the other day, and I think he would have wanted you to have it."

Claire hesitated before responding, "I don't know. The queen mother wouldn't like it if I left in the middle of the gala."

Maurelle raised her eyebrows. "Please. I promise not to keep you long. I feel as though we've had several…miscommunications throughout your stay, and I want to make it up to you."

Claire's mother had always told her to forgive and forget, so she supposed in the spirit of that she should say yes. "Okay, but only for a few minutes."

Maurelle nodded. "Of course." Then, she turned and led the way out of the Grand Ballroom.

Claire glanced at the clock again. *Nine thirty.* Ethan still hadn't appeared. Maybe he wouldn't show after all. Her shoulders sagged as she followed her stepmother toward the library, hoping they could make amends but unable to shake a feeling of trepidation.

After Claire entered the library, her eyes flew to the walls and walls of books. She'd love to sit in here one day with a cup of coffee and read the afternoon away. Distracted by this thought, she jumped at the sound of the door closing behind them. Claire spun around as the talking voices and clinking glasses faded away.

Maurelle stood about ten feet away beside a dusty stack of books. She waved Claire over. "Come here. I want to show you something."

A chill traveled down her spine, but she joined Maurelle.

Her stepmother placed a hand on one of the books and pulled downward. The entire section of the bookshelf moved inward, revealing a secret room.

She gasped.

Glancing at her, Maurelle asked, "Impressive, isn't it? Your father showed it to me shortly after we married. He used this room to store special things and to hide from time to time." She chuckled and walked into the stone-walled room.

Claire stared into the space but stood frozen. A cool draft from the hidden alcove made her shiver.

Maurelle lifted her head and met Claire's eyes. "Well, aren't you coming? I found one of your father's journals and thought you might want it."

Claire nodded and ducked her head, stepping into the room. She walked over to a rickety desk and chair that faced away from the room's doorway.

Her stepmother had yanked a string attached to a lightbulb overhead to illuminate the space. She pulled out the chair. "Take a seat. This is his journal." She tapped her red fingernail on the front of a dust-covered book resting on the desk.

Claire's curiosity trumped mistrust, so she walked to the chair and sat down. She blew off the book and opened it. The dust made her sneeze.

"Bless you," Maurelle said.

Claire opened the journal, and her eyes skimmed the front page. She responded a half-hearted, "Thank you," and barely noticed the lack of response from Maurelle. Flipping through the first several pages, Claire imagined her father sitting in this room, hiding away from the demands of royal life while putting his innermost thoughts to paper. After a few minutes, she closed the book and raised her head. Without turning around, her eyes still glued to the journal, she spoke, "I suppose we should return to the gala."

No one answered her.

Claire looked over her shoulder and realized she sat alone in the secret room. Maurelle had left. Jumping up from her seat, she flew to the closed door and pushed on it. It wouldn't budge. *No.* She banged on the door. *How could I be so foolish?* "Maurelle? Do you hear me? The door is locked. I can't get out. Let me out! Let me out! Help!" she screamed.

No response came. Claire banged on the door for what felt like an eternity. Maybe someone would pass by. What would she do now? If she didn't show at eleven for the big announcement, the queen mother might think she'd changed her mind—not to mention the midnight deadline that loomed. Slamming her palm against the door multiple times only resulted in a sore hand. Still no answer.

Who would come looking for her? The music from

the Royal Gala carried out of the Grand Ballroom and down the hallway and likely drowned out her cries for help. Claire imagined everyone dancing, chatting, eating—not searching in a dusty, old library for her. Even if someone wanted to find her, Claire doubted anyone knew about the existence of this secret room.

Scanning the room for something hard with which she could hit the door handle, Claire's eyes landed on a candlestick in the corner of the room. She walked over and picked it up, then returned to the door. Lifting it in both hands, she hammered it against the door handle over and over, praying one of the strikes might free her. After several blows, though, she tossed the candlestick to the ground, sank to the floor, and leaned her back against the door.

Frustration and fear settled around her like the dust covering everything in the room. Tears stung her eyes and spilled over, quickly turning to sobs. Claire cried, dropping her face into her hands. Is this how it all ended? Would she die in this room? After several minutes of weeping, she lifted her head. The journal sat on the desk across the room from her. Something within her soul nudged her to take a second look.

"Waste of time, but…at least I can learn more about my father," she spoke aloud.

Claire pushed herself up on one hand, taking care not to tear the skirt of her dress—not that it mattered at this point. The gala was over for her. Once standing, she rubbed her hands together, trying to remove the remnants of moisture from her tears and dirt from the candlestick. She walked to the desk and picked up the book. Flipping through its pages felt a bit like a violation of her father's privacy. Still, nosiness won out, and she dove into his thoughts.

The journal began around the time her father had met Claire's mother. Many of the pages held simple stories from their days together. One page read like a love letter to her mother that made Claire both blush and smile at the realization of the depth of their love.

Her fingers stopped on a page halfway through the book. Her father's handwriting looked shaky, and there were a few watermarks on the ink as if he'd been crying as he wrote the words. It looked like a letter he'd written but never sent.

> *My dearest Mona,*
>
> *I hope I dare to send this to you. It pains me to see you question your value in this place. I know the challenges a public life, much less a royal one, presents, but I beg you to reconsider. You bring light, love, and hope bless my life and the lives of those around you. I fear without you by my side the darkness in the world might win. No matter what you choose, know I will love you and pray for you forever.*
>
> *All of my love,*
> *Alexander*

Claire touched her hand to the page, stroking the broken promises...but perhaps they weren't broken. Maybe they mended themselves. She wished her mother had told her the truth about her father, and although it saddened Claire never to have known him in this life, she'd met him through his words after death.

Despite everything that had happened since her arrival at the castle, Claire didn't regret discovering her father. He'd reminded Claire of how her heavenly Father saw her—as a treasured child. It didn't matter if she became queen or pursued medicine or neither. Her worth went beyond all of that. Right now, she could let the darkness take over, or she could fight and pursue the light. Claire whispered, "I am a daughter of the King," and stood straighter.

She closed the book and glared at the door again. Maurelle would not defeat her. Claire would stand on the stage and claim her future as the queen of Amorley—even if she had to claw her way out of this room to get there.

She marched across the room and bent to retrieve the candlestick once more. *God, please send help.* Claire raised the candlestick high and banged on the door, then yelled, "Help! Help me. I'm in here. The door is stuck. Help."

She lifted the bludgeoner again and started to bring it down against the wood when the door swung open. Her jaw dropped at the appearance of her rescuer. "Ethan, what are you doing here? Never mind that. How did you find me?"

Ethan pulled the door open wider and scooped her into his strong arms. "I'm so glad you're okay. I asked your granny if she'd seen you, but we couldn't find you anywhere. Everyone I spoke with said they hadn't seen you for hours. I'm sorry I arrived late. I'd planned to be here by nine. Are you okay?" He released her and leaned back, inspecting her.

She nodded. "I'm fine…well, not fine; I'm a little traumatized. I thought that this secret room might become my tomb, but I decided I couldn't give up. Maurelle left me in there on purpose. Do you believe me?" She lifted her eyes to Ethan's concerned gaze.

His mouth settled into a grim line. "Yes, I do." He looked down at his wristwatch. "What time do you have to make your announcement?"

She frowned. "11:00 p.m. What time is it now?"

"10:55. If you want to make it, we'd better hurry to the ballroom."

She peered down at her sullied frock before meeting Ethan's gaze again. "I look terrible. I can't take the stage like this." She gestured with her hands down the length of her gown.

Ethan took her hand in his. "You can—you have to—besides, you always look beautiful."

Warmth filled Claire's cheeks, and she sent him a smile. "Thank you." Then, she drew in a deep breath before giving him a nod. "Okay, let's go." She followed Ethan out of the library and into the light of the hallway.

As they approached the entrance to the Grand Ballroom, Ethan turned around and said something. The buzz of voices and music filled the air, making it difficult for Claire to hear him.

"What?' she shouted, cupping her hands around her mouth.

He leaned closer and spoke in her ear, "Stay close to me. Let's go around the side and try to remain discreet. It may have been an accident that Maurelle let the door close behind you in that room, but I doubt it. It would be best if she didn't know you'd escaped."

Claire nodded her understanding and let Ethan guide her around the edge of the room. They stayed close to the draperies and as much in the shadows as possible. Once they made it toward the front corner of the room, Claire ducked behind Ethan's robust physique.

Her eyes skimmed the faces in the crowd searching for Maurelle.

Her stepmother stood at the opposite corner near the room's rear, holding a crystal flute in one hand and chatting happily with a gentleman. Claire couldn't see the man's face as he had his back turned.

The queen mother took the stage, and a hush fell across the crowd. She folded her hands in front of her and stood behind a clear podium with a microphone anchored to it. "Thank you again to everyone for attending this year's Royal Gala. As many of you know or have heard, tonight I'd hoped and planned to introduce to you the heir apparent to the Crown."

Ethan turned and gave Claire a nudge. "That's your cue."

The queen mother scanned the room and frowned. "Unfortunately—"

Claire rushed up the stairs to the stage, not bothering to worry about the possibility of tripping or how awful she must look after her rumble with dust bunnies in the library's secret room. She interrupted her grandmother, "Unfortunately, I'm a few minutes late and quite a mess. Please accept my apologies. I'd explain further—" Her eyes landed on Maurelle, who looked enraged at Claire's arrival "—but it's a long story. However, I want to make clear my intentions to accept the honor of heir apparent to the Crown of Amorley. This means that in a few months' time, I intend to participate in the Coronation Ceremony and become Amorley's next queen." Claire pressed on, "I have contacted someone in Parliament and have the assurance I can pursue medicine while ruling, which pleases me because I love helping patients. In the time I've spent here, I've grown to care deeply for Amorley and its people and learned more about my father. I'm proud to step into his shoes, and I believe if he stood before you today, he'd be so happy with this decision. I know how much he loved his country, and now I understand how much he would have loved me. I cannot think of a better marriage than joining those two things. Thank you for your time and for allowing me the opportunity to serve you." Claire stepped back from the podium, and the room erupted in applause.

Those people sitting in chairs around tables jumped to their feet, and the group started chanting, "Long live the queen. Long live the queen."

Claire's face burned, but she smiled, pleased at the room's reaction. She didn't know how the people would take the news that an outsider, a nobody, would become their queen. She glanced at the queen mother, and Claire did one of her awkward curtsies.

This time, Claire's grandmother cracked a grin and bowed her head in return. She walked over to join Claire and whispered in her ear, "Well done, dear. I'm proud of you and thankful that the Amorley people can look forward to a kind and intelligent queen. You will bring light to everything you do."

Claire nodded. "Thank you, Grandmother. I don't know if everyone feels that way." She flicked her eyes toward a scowling Maurelle. "But at least most people do."

Her grandmother leaned in once more, "Now, give them a polite wave as I taught you, and I believe I saw a handsome young man standing in the wings waiting for you. Better not keep him waiting." Then, the queen mother did something astounding—she winked.

Claire nearly fell over. She grinned. "You're right. Thank you." Waving for a few seconds to show her appreciation to the guests, Claire dropped her hand and hurried off the stage to the other side. All of her thoughts remained on reaching Ethan. She still had so much to tell him. Weaving her way around well-dressed ladies and gentlemen, Claire could see Ethan's head a few feet away—until a shoulder jutted in front of her, blocking her path.

"Well, well. I've underestimated you," Maurelle's syrupy smooth voice cooed. "I must say, I'm impressed by the speech you made. You didn't drop anything or trip. Of course, your dress," her eyes skimmed Claire's rumpled gown, "does leave something wanting. Did you roll around in the dirt again?"

Claire moved closer so only Maurelle could hear what she had to say. "You know what happened to my dress—the effects of being locked in that dusty, secret room. I can't believe you left me there."

Maurelle threw a hand to her chest. "Me? Leave you there on purpose? My dear, what a crazy story to concoct. The way I recall the incident, I took you there to give you a beloved possession of your father's, which I thought you would cherish. We chatted for a few moments, then I got called away. I told you to follow me, but you must have been so engrossed in your father's journal that you didn't hear me. I didn't know you hadn't exited the room. With so many people attending the gala, I assumed you were floating around here somewhere. You can't blame me if you made an error in judgment and lost focus."

Claire's heartbeat pounded in her ears. She clenched her fists at her sides. "You cannot expect me to believe that story, can you?"

Maurelle lifted a fingernail and tapped it on Claire's chest. "I do. You'll find if you share such a preposterous story with others at the castle, they'll think you've gone mad, and that would make you unfit, dare I say, unworthy to wear the Crown. Now, that would be a shame, wouldn't it? Then, my darling son might have to take over. No, I think it's best for everyone involved if this little misunderstanding remains between us."

Claire planted her hands on her hips. "Maurelle, I do hope it was an accident that you locked me in that room, but either way, I'm going to become queen. If I told the story to the queen mother, she might have a surprising take on it. Perhaps, what would be best for everyone is if you went on a holiday. Maybe to the summer castle? I hear it's lovely with its gardens and landscapes. Either way, I'm not leaving, and I'm not giving up the Crown. Not today, not tomorrow, not ever. Light always triumphs over darkness, and I know my worth, and it doesn't reside in what you or other people think." With her final words, Claire spun around and started to walk away from her stepmother.

The daunting voice called once more, "Oh, Claire."

Claire looked back over her shoulder. "What?"

A sinister smile spread across Maurelle's lips. "Ask Ethan's father why he's so opposed to his son being with you. I'll let you in on a secret, it's not simply because he wants Abigail's fortune. Ask him why he wouldn't be thrilled to see his son marry the future queen." Her stepmother turned around and sashayed away.

As Claire watched Maurelle retreat, she couldn't help but think their war had only begun. Still, she released a sigh of relief at winning this battle. Claire looked toward Ethan with hesitancy. As much as she hated to admit it, nagging concern grew deep within Claire. Why wouldn't Ethan's father want to see his son married to the Crown? Maurelle did make a point. *Well...only one way to find out.* She'd have to face them both and confront Ethan's father.

The two Kane men appeared to be in a heated discussion. Ethan wore a frown and a furrowed brow. His father kept slamming one fist into the other hand and then pointing at Ethan's chest.

Claire lifted her chin, squared her shoulders, and marched over to Ethan and his father. As she slid next to Ethan, he put a protective arm across her shoulder. She looked at Ethan's father and asked, "May I interrupt?"

He glared in response. "There's nothing to interrupt because I'm done with this conversation. I told my son that his time of putting off family responsibilities has come to an end. I don't suppose he's enlightened you about his future, but he remains betrothed to Abigail Fulton. I came here tonight to remind him of that. Abigail and her family are here as well, and I urged Ethan not to make a spectacle of himself. I won't let him destroy everything his family has worked hard to build."

Claire glanced at Ethan, and he looked like flames might shoot out of his eyes at any moment. She returned her attention to James Kane. "Sir, I knew about the situation with Abigail, and I only want happiness for Ethan, but I don't believe Abigail will make him happy. I could, though. In fact, we would bring one another a great deal of happiness."

His father leaned closer and put a finger in her face. He lowered his voice and hissed, "Listen to me. I don't care who you are or if you become the queen of the world. My son will never marry you. Never. Do you understand?"

His affront startled her, and she pulled back. "What do you mean? Why would you object so fiercely to a union between the two of us? I come from a royal bloodline, and my family has wealth, maybe not as much as Abigail's, but still a great deal. I'm a physician, I work hard, and I'm the heir to the Crown. What could make you hate my family and me so much?"

He spat out his answer, "Your father stole something from me years ago, and I will never forget it."

She raised a brow. "You knew my father? Like when you were kids?"

Ethan's father narrowed his eyes. "I knew your father for many years. We were close friends until I started dating an American woman visiting Amorley for her study abroad. Once he saw her, he decided he had to have her for himself. Alexander always got everything he wanted, and if he didn't, he'd take yours."

Claire's eyes widened.

The duke seemed pleased at her shock. "Oh, you're surprised. You thought your father was a saint?" He shook his head. "I'm afraid he was no saint...in fact, he betrayed me and our friendship the day he stole the love of my life. I've never forgiven him for it, and I don't intend to see my son marry the daughter of the object of Alexander's affection."

Claire's mouth dropped open. "You loved my mother? That's what this is about?"

Glaring again, Ethan's father spat, "It's about betrayal. As long as I have breath in my lungs, I'll never approve of a marriage between my son and the Crown. Your family has caused me pain for the final time. I forbid it. Ethan has a choice to make—you or his family and the Kane inheritance."

Shaking her head, Claire pleaded, "You can't do that to him. It wasn't my mother's fault—not really. I can't help how things transpired between you and my father years ago. Please." She lifted her eyes to Ethan, unsure of what to say to him.

Ethan clenched his jaw, and his face filled with blood. "Father, I love my family. I do. I don't want to hurt mother or dishonor either of you. But, I have to listen to my heart. If I have to choose between love and title, I choose Claire. Every time. I'm in love with her, and she's the most wonderful woman I've ever known. I pray that someday you'll find a way to forgive her father for the past and me for this disappointment. I love Claire, and I'll never marry Abigail. I'm sorry, but you'll have to hang your expectations on Richard's shoulders."

James Kane stepped closer to his son. With only inches separating them, he gave Ethan an even stare. "You're making a huge mistake." Then, he stormed off, probably to mend relations with the Fulton family and convince Richard to take Ethan's place as his family's great hope.

Ethan turned to face Claire, placing gentle hands on

her shoulders. "Are you okay? I'm sorry about that. What terrible things to hear about your father. I'm sure it's not true."

She met his gaze, and warmth filled her chest. "I'm fine. I feel terrible about the strife between you and your father. I can't do anything about the past—mine or my father's. All I can do is look toward the future."

Ethan closed the distance between him and Claire, gathering her in his arms. He leaned his head near her ear, whispering, "I couldn't agree more." He held her close for several minutes and then released her, taking her hands in his. "I have something important to ask you."

She grinned and raised a brow. "You do?" Her hands quivered, and she tried to steady them.

He nodded, sending her a warm smile. "I do." Ethan knelt on one knee, still holding her hands in his, and then lifted his head, staring into her eyes.

Thinking she might melt looking into the blue pools that seemed to pierce her soul, she tried not to swoon as she'd seen in movies. She pulled in a deep breath and released it, along with all her doubts and insecurities.

Ethan's face became serious. "Dr. Claire Thomson, future Queen of Amorley, I love you. You're the most beautiful, smart, and kind woman I've ever known. I don't care about anything that happened in the past— the newspaper photo, our argument, any of it. I only want light and happiness for you. I want to see you serve the people of Amorley and pursue your passion for medicine. I want you to have it all. It would be an honor to spend the rest of my life showing you how worthy and loved you are to me. I promise to slay all the dragons that come our way and put God and you first always. Claire, would you do me the honor of becoming my wife?"

Claire's heart pounded, and butterflies danced in her stomach. Happy tears brimmed to the surface of her eyes, and she nodded. "Yes. A million times, yes. I love you, too, Ethan. I'm sorry for everything I said. I was upset about Milo, but I shouldn't have taken it out on you. Coming here has changed my life—for the better. It's shown me who I am and how strong I can be. It doesn't matter that I didn't know my father in this life because I have my heavenly Father to look out for me and a lot of wonderful people here on earth, too. I'm so thankful for Granny, the queen mother and Albert, and especially for you. So, yes. Yes, I'll marry you."

Ethan's grin widened, and he rose from his position. He picked up Claire, lifting her feet from the ground, and spun her in a circle before setting her down again. "You've made me the happiest man." Gazing into her eyes, he took her face in both of his hands and tilted her chin toward his. He caressed her cheek with his thumb and searched her eyes. Leaning closer, he grazed her lips with his and whispered, "I love you, Claire, and I always will."

She inhaled, breathing in his scent of amber and musk. A shiver traveled down her neck and coursed through her arms, and her pulse quickened. She murmured, "I love you, Ethan."

Then, Ethan pressed his lips against hers, gently at first, chasing away all the fears she'd had about the future and her place in the royal world. His kisses intensified, and Claire melted into them, knowing this man would protect her heart at any cost.

His lips lingered after the last kiss, and as he pulled

away, Claire's tiara fell to the ground. "Allow me," he offered, bending down to retrieve it. He picked it up and stood, handing it to her.

She accepted it and sent him a grin. "Thanks." Claire placed it on her head and asked, "How does it look?"

"Your tiara's tilted."

Her hands flew up to her head and tried to adjust it, but one side of it had caught in her hair.

"Want me to help?" he asked.

She nodded. "Please."

As he released the tendril of hair that had snagged on one of the glittering jewels, he tucked the loose strand behind her ear. "It looks like you won't have to pick between wearing a stethoscope or a tiara."

She laughed and shook her head. "I won't. Thanks to you." The music from the string quartet swelled, and couples around them moved to the dance floor in pairs.

Ethan extended a hand to her. "May I have this dance?"

She placed her hand in his and found his gaze. "Yes."

He took her in his arms and moved her around the dance floor, swaying to the music. Claire rested her head on his shoulder. "I know after everything that transpired with you
father and my stepmother, we might face more trouble in the future. As long as we have one another and God, we can conquer anything." She raised her head and smiled.

He nodded and whispered, "Anything," and his lips found hers once more.

When she parted from his kiss, her eyes caught

sight of Granny standing next to Albert at the side of the room.

Granny sent Claire a wink and a thumbs-up.

She chuckled.

Ethan smiled and raised a brow. "What's so funny?"

Claire shrugged. "Granny."

Ethan nodded, understanding without further explanation.

Staring into his eyes, she realized she no longer felt royally confused. Now, Claire's heart knew her worth and only felt one thing—royally in love.

Epilogue
One Month Later

Claire walked out the rear entrance of Evercliff Castle to the Royal Gardens and
breathed in the fragrance of lavender and roses. She smiled and took the stone steps down to the pebbled path.

Ethan stood waiting for her below, a wide grin taking residence on his face.

Claire gave him a quick peck on the lips and smiled again. "You look happy. I read your note this morning. What did you want to show me?"

He stared down at her as he stroked her hair with one hand. "The past few months have seemed spectacular, but I realize they've been hard, too. What happened to Milo…well, I know how heartbroken it left you."

She nodded. "It did."

Ethan continued, "I wanted to do something to mend that heartbreak."

Searching his face, she asked, "What did you do?"

He shook his head. "It's a surprise. Close your eyes."

Claire obeyed. She could feel him waving a hand in front of her face.

"Are they closed? No peeking," he ordered with a teasing voice.

She bobbed her head. "They're closed. Promise."

"Okay, stand here and don't move. I'll be right back."

Claire stood still with her eyes closed for at least a minute before she heard his footsteps return.

"Still closed?" he asked.

"Yes," she answered, shifting her weight.

"Okay, on the count of three, you can open them. Ready?"

"Ready," she answered.

Ethan made some rustling noises, and it sounded like he set something at her feet. "One, two, three. Open your eyes."

When Claire opened them, the most adorable, blond golden retriever puppy sat before her wearing a sapphire and gold bow tie.

He tipped his head to the side as if sizing her up. Then, he gave a tiny bark and stood, tail wagging.

Claire's throat tightened, and tears sprang to her eyes. She bent down and stroked the sweet ball of fur, cooing at him.

The puppy leapt on her, nearly knocking her over, and Claire laughed. As she continued to pet her new friend, she found Ethan's gaze. "Is he for me?"

Ethan beamed and nodded. "Yep. He's your new puppy. Thought you could use some backup within the castle walls. What do you think?"

Tears trailed down her cheeks, and she grinned. "Thank you. Thank you so much. I love him. And you. I love you, too." She jumped up and wrapped her arms around Ethan.

Ethan bent his head down and planted a soft, warm kiss on her lips.

The puppy barked, startling them, and Claire's head sprang back. She laughed, and Ethan joined her.

He stared into her eyes and asked, "Are you happy?"

With Coronation Day on the horizon and a wedding to plan, Claire didn't think anything could make her ever-after any happier than the gift of Ethan's love and her new furry friend. Fresh tears fell, and Claire nodded. "I am…I truly am."

THE END

Newsletter signup:
https://www.jillboyceauthor.com/contact-1

Hook for the next book:
How will Claire handle royal life as she prepares for her coronation and a wedding that may not happen? Find out what happens next in the Royal Medicine Series by staying in touch here: **www.jillboyceauthor.com**

Also by Jill Boyce:

Harte Broken

About the Book:

Time doesn't heal all wounds. Love does.

Amy Harte, an Emergency Medicine physician, lost her mother to cancer suddenly on the day of her residency graduation one year ago. As a doctor, she struggles with not being able to save her mother and experiencing her best day on her worst. Since then, she has turned from her relationship with God in her guilt and grief. Near the fateful day's anniversary, her father calls to tell Amy the bank may take her childhood home. Amy knows she must save the house that holds the last precious memories of her mother.

Meanwhile, Amy meets a gorgeous Christian man, Seth, who slowly restores her belief in love and God's goodness. Their happily ever after may have to wait because Dr. Mark Blakely, Amy's dashing hospital colleague, has never met a woman he couldn't woo. Still, Amy suspects Mark values the chase more than her heart. Time is running out for Amy to save her family home and release her anger and guilt. Will she discover that love, especially God's love, heals all wounds?

Sneak Peek the First Chapter:

Psalm 147:3 He heals the brokenhearted and binds up
their wounds.

Chapter 1
July 2, 2017, Sunday

Amy Harte stared at the brass nameplate in front of
her as she knelt on the cool green lawn. She ran her fingers
over the letters, tracing the precious name. Her gaze shifted
to the tilted vase attached to her mother's headstone, and she
reached out to straighten it. A light breeze blew past,
carrying the sharp scent of freshly cut grass.

"I'm sorry, Mom. I'm so sorry." Only silence
answered. She drew in a shuddering breath. Today marked
an anniversary she never wanted to celebrate. One year ago,
Amy had graduated from residency and fulfilled a lifelong
dream to become a physician—but on that same day, she lost
her mother. How does one celebrate when the best day of life
is also the worst?

Guilt washed over Amy as she reflected on how
she'd let her mother down. She'd missed being with her
when she passed and still carried the burden of failure to
save her mom despite being a physician tasked with healing
others.

The phone call Amy had received earlier that
morning from her father rose in her thoughts. "Hello," she'd
mumbled.

"Amy? Did I wake you?" Her father's low-timbered
voice bellowed.

"Dad, are you okay?" Amy rubbed the sleep out of her eyes
and tried to gain her bearings.

"Yes," her dad's voice trailed off.

"What's going on?" The last year's events flashed

through her mind, and she felt a rock developing in the pit of her stomach.

"It's about the house. I got a call Friday morning from the bank and met with the manager."

Amy ran a hand through her hair, relaxing a bit. "Dad, you haven't had a mortgage in years."

"Well, that's true. We did pay it off a few years ago."

"Okay, so then what's the problem?"

"The problem is that because of the cost of your mom's treatments and then the funeral, I had to take out a second mortgage on the house. I didn't know what else to do…"

She frowned. "So, what does this mean? Can't we ask the bank for an extension? I'm sure they'll understand."

"They understand, but that doesn't change the fact that the bill is due. The bank manager said that I have sixty days to come up with the rest of the loan, $50,232, or the house will go to foreclosure," his voice cracked.

She could tell he was close to tears. "Oh, Dad. Don't cry. We'll figure something out." Amy wracked her brain, calculating her student loan balance, which teetered over the six-figure mark, and considered her rent and car payment. She just started working at Metropolitan Hospital, so her savings account was anemic.

"They can't take your home." She'd had tea parties there with her mother. It was where she had learned to ride a bike and gotten ready for prom. "Where would you live?" Amy tried to conceal the rising panic in her voice.

"Don't worry about me. The money from my pension more than covers my monthly living expenses, and I'm sure I could find something reasonable to rent."

"No. Absolutely not. We lost mom. We can't lose the family home."

"Well, if you come up with a way to make fifty-grand in the next sixty days, let me know. Otherwise, I think it would be a good idea if you came over in the next few weeks to go through things."

"Don't start packing up yet, Dad. I love you." Amy hung up and made a silent vow to save her childhood home.

A butterfly landed on her hand, snapping Amy out of the memory. Hot tears stung her eyes, and a single droplet rolled down her cheek. She wiped it away and shook her head. No time for tears today. She stood and brushed tiny blades of grass off her faded mint-green scrub pants.

A grey-haired older gentleman dressed in overalls stood a few feet away, raking mulch into a flowerbed. "You've got to receive God's forgiveness sometime, young lady." He continued his work as he spoke, not lifting his head.

Amy stood straighter and pressed her lips into a firm line. "Excuse me, what did you say?"

The stranger halted his task and rested his arm on the rake. His eyes found Amy's. "I said, you're going to have to accept God's forgiveness…only way to move forward. Guilt will eat you up inside and make it hard to love and live." The man shrugged and resumed his work as if never a word was spoken.

Her mouth fell open. *What does he know about God's forgiveness? He's probably crazy.* She started to refute his intrusion, but her pager beeped, reminding her to get moving. She walked to her car and hopped inside.

The muggy summer air, combined with choking grief, made breathing difficult. She cranked up the air conditioning and drove across town, arriving at the parking lot of Scottsburg, Virginia's community hospital. She stopped the car, stamped down the emergency brake, and paused. "Come on, Amy. Get it together. You're a professional." She slid out of the car and walked toward the hospital with hurried steps.

Straightening her shoulders, Amy stepped past the main glass doors of Metropolitan Hospital and entered the five-star, luxury-hotel-like foyer. Despite the crystal chandelier hanging overhead and a white marble floor below, the classic scent of bleach revealed it to be a well-endowed medical facility with an expansive, wealthy board of directors and donors.

Amy strode into the Emergency Department and sent a nod to her best friend and lead respiratory therapist. "Hey Beth, how's it looking today? Swamped already?"

Beth, petite with shoulder-length blond hair, leaned against the central nursing station, the main activity hub. She flicked her hand with a quick wave and grinned. "Hey, Amy!"   Glancing at the large whiteboard filled with patients' names and room assignments confirmed her assessment.

Blowing her bangs out of her eyes, Beth nodded her head. "Yeah, it's been a madhouse. I thought people slept in on Sundays."

"I suppose some people use Sundays to get things done. You know… laundry, dishes, late brunches, grocery store runs… or go to church, I guess."

Some people, but not Amy. Tears threatened to spill over again, but she turned her head away and forced them back down. She held her breath. A gentle hand settled on her arm, and
Amy met Beth's sympathetic eyes.

"Hey, do you need to go home? I know this must be a hard day for you. If you want, I can tell them you didn't feel well."

She gulped in a fresh breath of air and exhaled. Amy shook her head. "No, I'm fine." As she reached for a chart, the overhead paging system announced an incoming emergency.

An ambulance siren blared, and two EMTs burst through the ED's double doors.

Amy rushed toward them.

The first medic rattled off statistics. "Victim is Brian

Broadstone, driver in a two-car motor vehicle accident. He suffered a head trauma and suspected concussion, with a laceration to the right scalp. Vitals are stable."

She shifted her eyes from the patient to the medic. "Thanks, I'll take it from here." She grabbed her stethoscope from her neck and began her exam. After finding the patient in stable condition, she sent him to get a head CT.

The emergency department double doors parted again, and a tall, handsome man with dark brown hair burst through them. His eyes widened as he saw Brian's stretcher roll away.

"Hey, where's my brother going?"

He wore a black short sleeve t-shirt stretched snugly across his broad chest and thick shoulders and flattered his fit physique. His chiseled jaw clenched, and concern clouded his chestnut eyes.

Amy's cheeks warmed, and she blinked hard. *Pay attention.* She shook her head, gathering her thoughts. "Hi, I'm Dr. Amy Harte. Your brother's stable, but I sent him off for imaging. A head injury warrants a thorough workup. Were you in the car with him?" She smiled, hoping to ease his worry.

"Yeah, sorry I'm late. I rode over in the ambulance but stepped outside for a minute to call my dad. I didn't want my parents to hear about the accident from someone else."

Nodding her head, Amy understood. She knew how Scottsburg's rumor mill operated.

The handsome man met Amy's gaze, and his serious expression relaxed as he took a few steps closer. "Is he going to be okay?"

"I think he'll be fine, but I don't want to miss anything. Are you okay? We can evaluate you, too."

"I'm fine. Not a scratch on me." He stretched his hand toward Amy. "I should introduce myself. My name is Seth."

She shook his hand, and a shiver traveled down her

spine at his touch. Releasing his grip, she cleared her throat. "Nice to meet you. If your brother's tests are normal, then he may be able to go home tonight as long as someone stays with him." Amy attempted to keep her tone even and professional. "Where were you guys headed so early this morning?"

The good-looking stranger grinned and shifted his weight. "Well, this week is our mother's birthday, so we were headed to grab breakfast, then take in the early church service so we'd have time to get things together afterward for her big day."

She raised her brow. "Did you make it to breakfast?"

Seth shook his head. "No, we didn't. Come to think of it, I'm starving. Do you think I have time to run to the cafeteria and grab something before Brian gets back?"

Amy smiled and nodded. "Sure. That's fine. I'll let him know where you went. If you're like me, it's hard to function before coffee."

Seth nodded. "Same." Seth searched her face, his eyes warm with interest. "Would you like a cup? I'll bring you one back."

Amy's cheeks burned, and her palms grew damp. Her fingertips tingled. She longed to say yes, but she feared that the names on the whiteboard were multiplying by the minute.

Someone tapped her on the shoulder. She turned, and Dr. Mark Blakely stood with two foam cups in hand.

Mark wore a confident grin as he eyed Seth. "No worries. I've got it covered." He passed one of the cups to Amy.

She hesitated, then accepted it. "Thanks, Mark."

Disappointment flashed across Seth's face for a moment. "Okay. Thanks again for taking great care of my brother." He smiled and reached out to shake Amy's hand again. "I'll be right back." Seth turned and walked away.

Mark left Amy's side to attend to another incoming patient.

Amy wished she could have talked to Seth longer, but Mark had impeccable timing.

Mark asked her out on a date weekly, despite her lack of encouragement. She suspected Dr.

Blakely's dating record included most of the female population of Scottsburg.

Amy approached Beth standing at the nursing station and noticed an unmistakable smirk on her best friend's face. "So, I see you've met the new Chief Financial Officer."

Exhaling for the first time in a minute, Amy asked, "What do you mean?"

Beth's grin widened, and she crossed her arms in front of her chest. "Seth Broadstone. The charge nurse told me your patient's brother is the new CFO of the hospital. Apparently, he started a few weeks ago. So, this should be interesting. I saw the look between the two of you." She winked.

Amy rolled her eyes. "I don't know what you're talking about…there was no look. Besides, right now, I don't have time to date anybody. I have a lot on my mind." Her thoughts drifted to the conversation she'd had with her dad about her parent's house. "I'm channeling all my energy into work." She owed it to her mom.

Beth's face fell, and she grew serious. "Hey, I get it. Your work is your life…but don't forget to make time for some fun, too. I guess we hadn't met Seth yet because he's stationed on the floor with the administrators."

Shrugging in nonchalance, Amy agreed, "You're probably right." She secretly hoped this wouldn't be the last time their paths crossed.

Author Biography:

Jill writes inspirational romantic fiction with a medical theme. Her debut novels are part of the *A Dose of Love* series. Each story can stand alone, but all feature strong female leads facing challenging life circumstances while finding love along the way. Jill's love of romance and her experience of losing her mother on the same day of her daughter's birth inspired the first novel, *Harte Broken*. It raises the question, "What happens when the best day is also the worst one?"

Royally Confused, Book One in the *Royal Medicine Series* introduces Claire Thomson, the heroine physician who must discover her worth by finding out her true identity. Jill enjoys royal romances and wanted to create a contemporary world filled with classic fairy-tale characters—a knight in shining armor, an evil Queen, and yes, a princess. Of course, Claire slays her own dragons and learns she comes from the one true King, her heavenly Father, who declares her worthy and loved. This series will follow the characters forward in the fictional royal world of Amorley.

Jill is a physician and mom, who loves coffee, travel, and anything glittered. She treasures spending time with her husband and children, who are her heart and greatest joy.

Let's stay in touch! Follow me on:

Facebook to enjoy #fun, faith, hope…and a little coffee!
Jill Boyce, Author, LLC

Check out my **website**— www.jillboyceauthor.com to join
my monthly **newsletter** and hear about my puppy's latest
hijinks, new releases, discounts, giveaways, and other great
deals!

Connect with me on **Twitter** or **Instagram** as well!

Join me on **Goodreads** and **BookBub** to find out what I'm
reading!

Books By Jill Boyce

A DOSE OF LOVE SERIES

Harte Broken (Book One)
Perfectly Imperfect (Book Two
A Prescription for Beauty (Book Three)